M000296456

The Tarot Mysteries by Bevan Atkinson

The Empress Card
The High Priestess Card
The Magician Card
The Fool Card

THE MAGICIAN CARD

A Tarot Mystery

by

Bevan Atkinson

ISBN 978-0-9969425-1-5

Acknowledgements

Thanks to my writing cheerleaders, especially my cousin Nancey Brackett, and former English teacher Dr. Karl Harshbarger, who both helped me get going again when I was stuck.

Thanks also to my lovely friend Barb Thompson, to the marvelously detail-oriented Chris and Dianne, and to Duane Unkefer for his manuscript expertise and always useful advice, plus whenever I call he always asks me what I'm wearing. And of course a shout-out to Mr. Hitchcock.

For James Atkinson and Barbara Louise

". . . The Tarot . . . may have been originally intended, by an unknown Maker, to be used . . . as an intellectual and intuitive system, for making systems, for destroying them, and for creating."
— Bill Butler, *Dictionary of the Tarot*

"Our remedies oft in ourselves do lie
Which we ascribe to heaven."
— William Shakespeare, *All's Well That Ends Well*

≈1≈

I was taking one last sip of my now cold peppermint tea. It was Monday morning, between the breakfast rush and the lunch hour crush, and there were mostly empty tables at Enrico's on Broadway. The woman whose tarot cards I had read was gone, happier now, feeling free to make a decision that had stymied her.

"Do you read for strangers?" he asked me, a young man of medium height, with longish straight dark brown hair, bright black eyes, olive complexion. He was slender, nervous. He was wearing a black T-shirt and dark gray stovepipe jeans. Androgynous, but San Francisco calls itself "everybody's favorite city," and that goes triple if you're androgynous.

He had been sitting at the table next to mine but had risen when the woman did and was facing me now. He spoke in a light tenor and gripped the back of an empty chair at the side of my table, shoulders shrugged upward as he leaned toward me, his gaze intent.

"Sometimes," I said.

"How much do you charge?"

"I don't. It's nice if you can do something in kind for me, if you think the reading has been helpful."

"Really? You don't charge anything? Why not?"

"I don't make my living this way. I read for people who ask me to. It's a gift, to be able to read the cards, and I pass it along. I do believe it keeps things in balance if the people I read for respond with something of value, but I leave it up to them. Sometimes all they can manage is to thank me, and that's fine."

"Could you read my cards now? Do you have time?"

I watched him, and waited for my intuition to kick in. I didn't get the feeling he was trying to pick me up. *He's all right,* my inner voice told me, *and there will be contradictions.*

"Please sit down," I said, gesturing at the chair he was white-knuckling, "wherever you like."

"I'll get my coffee," he said, swiveling and

picking up his cappuccino from the next table. The normally nonstop traffic up and down Broadway was intermittent. Right now there were mostly cars instead of rumbling trucks.

Since the irreparably damaged double-decker Embarcadero Freeway, including the Broadway off-ramp, was torn down after the 1989 earthquake, traffic is much quieter around Enrico's. The café empties out in the late morning and I don't feel like I am taking up a table a paying patron would occupy. I never read cards at Mama's for instance, which is always packed, with a line outside waiting patiently for the exceptional omelettes.

As it has been for many years, Broadway is a mix of strip clubs and restaurants on the edge of North Beach, the former headquarters of all things beatnik. Enrico's is just around the corner from City Lights Bookstore, run by Lawrence Ferlinghetti, where I shop when I feel the urge to buy subversive, or just plain unusual, literature.

Some years ago the Condor, once the home of Carol Doda and the original topless review, had taken down the huge sign of the nude woman with her blinking red-light nipples. At the time it was scheduled to be replaced by a sign showing just the name of the club, some people fought to keep the nude lady; they said she was a landmark and should be preserved.

I love my nutty city.

There was a big man sitting across the café by himself. Not at all fat, just very large. He looked over at me briefly and when our eyes met I felt color rising into my cheeks. He looked away, a smile turning up the corners of his mouth.

The slender man sat down across from me and immediately picked up his cup, holding it with both hands, his fingers long and smooth. I had the impression that with those hands he could do something complicated, and he would do it adroitly.

He took a sip of his coffee.

"I was watching you read that woman's cards," he said, looking at me. His dark eyes glittered with intelligence, and he tilted his head with curiosity.

"I could tell you helped her."

"How could you tell?"

"The way she stood up. Like she had a purpose. And she looked light-hearted when she walked away."

I nodded my head.

"That's what a reading is supposed to do for you. Make you feel unstuck, and recognized, and free from whatever has you stalled. Have you had your cards read before?"

"No,"

"May I ask, why now?"

"Because I don't know what to do," he said, and lifted his hands to cover his face. He shook his head like a dog shaking off raindrops.

Sliding his fingertips down to rest on his cheekbones, he looked at me and said, "I can't figure out what's happening. And I can't figure out how to…," he paused and thought, "…how to maneuver."

One hand wriggled like an eel, back and forth toward me across the table.

I looked at him, then away toward the late morning sky beyond the patio. I paid attention to how I felt about him and what he was saying. I felt safe. I wanted to do what I could to help him.

Unlike most people, who have been taught to mistrust and avoid using their intuition, I rely on mine utterly. People tell me I am too trusting. What they are really saying is that they do not know how to trust properly, using the innate skills they are born with to assess whether strangers intend evil or good.

"I'm Alexandra Bard," I said, turning back to him and holding out my hand. "People call me Xana."

He shook hands with me, firmly but without smashing my fingers against my rings. His skin was very smooth. I didn't feel any spark of warning from the handshake.

"I'm Asa Ballantine."

"You and I are going to work together on this, okay? A card reading is not a test, and I'm not going to talk about long voyages or dark strangers or coming into a lost inheritance. The tarot is a tool to get at information you and I might not otherwise notice or remark on.

"I'm going to tell you what I think," I went on, "and then based on your reactions and comments we'll try to unearth information that will shine enough light on your circumstances that you feel free to decide, or move, or act, or maybe do nothing. If I'm doing this properly what you will mostly feel is recognized. How does that sound to you?"

"Great. Wonderful. Thank you."

"Take the cards," I said, handing them to him. "Work with them until you think they're ready."

"Can I look at them?"

"Sure. Whatever you feel like doing."

"How will I know when they're ready?"

"You'll just know. Take all the time you want."

I sat and cleared my mind while he shuffled. Inwardly I said the prayer I always say when I read the cards for someone: *Please let Your light shine through me clearly, undimmed, unaltered.*

"They're big," he said.

"This particular deck is."

"Are there smaller ones?"

"Sure. And many different designs. There's a version of the tarot in just about every culture around the world."

I knew to keep my tarot explanation general

and to a minimum; most people are preoccupied with their problems and uninterested in Court de Ghibellin and the Temple of Karnak, or the confab of Magi in Fez during the sixth century, or Louis XIII and the tarot's emergence in the fourteenth century as the Marseille deck, brought by Gypsies who entered France from the Mediterranean. People are not generally fascinated about the fact that Gypsies are so called because they were thought to have come from Egypt.

There's lore, tons of lore. Nobody cares. People who ask me to read their cards don't want to learn the history of the occult sciences, the links between Jung's theory of archetypes and the images on the tarot cards, nor do they want to discover the secret to world peace. They want answers to personal questions about love, or jobs, or money, or health, or family.

But I haven't yet read cards for a Miss America contestant, so world peace may still come up as a question someday.

Asa spread out the cards face up on the silk scarves that I use as protectors and tablecloths. Looking at the designs, he picked up the Nine of Swords.

"This one is sad," he said.

"It can be, yes."

In the best known tarot deck, called the Rider-Waite pack, the Nine of Swords card shows a robed figure sitting up in bed, hands covering the face as if the person were weeping. I use a different deck, in which the Nine of Swords shows multiple hands emerging from clouds, with the hands holding nine swords. That Asa could read sadness into such a non-figurative image was telling, to me anyway.

I waited to see what else he would say about the card, but he was quiet. He replaced it and shuffled the cards capably with his long, elegant fingers. Most people fumble around a little—not he. He held the pack for a moment, bending his head and concentrating, and then held it out across the table to me.

"Done," he said. I didn't take the cards from him.

"Split them into three piles, please."

He stared at the cards as he separated them and set three piles down on the silk. He looked up at me.

I studied the piles for a moment, waiting to see which one wanted to be picked up. My hand went to the pile to my left. I stacked the other two and set them aside.

I began laying out the Celtic Cross, a ten-card layout that curls outward from a center card and is intended to provide a general overview of any Querent's situation, a Querent being the person for whom you are reading.

The center card was The Magician. Crossing it was The Emperor. The Background card was the

Nine of Swords, the card Asa had called "sad." Just Passing was The High Priestess. The Crowning card was Death, followed by the Ten of Swords in the Soon-To-Come spot. The Tower Card turned up in the Fear position of the layout. Others' Influence was The Hermit, reversed, meaning upside-down. Querent's Hope was the Seven of Pentacles. Outcome was the Five of Wands.

I had never seen a layout like it and I pray I never will again.

"Holy God in heaven above me," I said.

I steadied myself, took a deep breath, let it out, and looked up at him.

"You're at war," I said, back in control and using my soft, tarot reader voice. It's the voice late-night FM radio deejays use, and I fall into it when I'm doing a reading. Asa looked frightened, and then he nodded slowly.

"God help your enemies," I said, calm now but appalled as well, holding his gaze. "God is already helping you, and you need all the help you can get."

≈2≈

Agatha stared at the sign on the door of the Twin's Armoire and slumped. *Oh that is just fine,* she thought. *Rolf gives me money for a new outfit and you are closed today. Now what am I to do?*

She stood for a moment, gazing sadly at the sign. When she set out for Nob Hill she had been happy to see that it was such a beautiful morning. No rain today and a nice day to walk, even up and down Nob Hill. She was sorry that she would have to spend the rest of the sunny day in her house instead of outdoors.

I will just start the chicken marinating, she thought. *And I should wash down the front steps and prune the roses. It is cold enough they are dormant now, or as dormant as they ever get here. I can feed them and they will be so pretty this summer when Rolf looks out the window of his office.*

She resented the wasted trip, but she would just have to come up with time tomorrow. It was always a challenge to find time for herself in the day, and even with Rolf's permission to go shopping she had felt a twinge of guilt about the time away that she should have spent on the house, on making things look exactly the way Rolf liked them to look.

She was surprised when he gave her money this morning and told her to go out and shop; he hadn't done that in months. "Buy zumting pretty," he had said in his Teutonic English, "and have lunch downtown mit a friend."

Only sometimes, when he was a little *beschwipst* on schnapps, would he permit himself to lapse into German with her. Speaking English was a necessary discipline for him, he insisted, and for her as well. Sometimes when he couldn't think of the English word he would become angry, and she would have to find an excuse to leave the room quickly before something unpleasant happened.

Suggesting she have lunch with a friend was an odd thing for Rolf to do, though. He knew very well she had lost touch with her friends over the years; his demands on her time and attention, and his unpleasantness when someone stopped by for a visit, had gradually driven her few friends out of her life. Today she couldn't think of a soul to call on such short notice.

Even so, she had imagined she might wander through Neiman-Marcus and up to the restaurant on the top floor. She remembered that they had the most delicious rolls, with an oversized pat of chilled butter on a spotless white plate. She remembered that there had been a time when such treats were more frequent.

She looked up and down the street in case the twin sisters showed up. They were so attentive to their customers, and the styles they carried were always unique. Shopping at the Twin's Armoire was not like shopping in a big department store, where you paid too much for something anyone might buy. If she was going to pay a premium, the outfit should be only for her to wear.

Another day, she said to herself and walked back to the parking lot under the Masonic Auditorium. *I will find a way to have time to myself twice instead of once.*

Rolf had even let her take the car. She started the Mercedes and turned on the radio. She had tuned it to the classical station for the drive downtown. She would have to remember to switch it back to talk radio with all those mean men and women yelling about liberals when she got home, and she would have to put the driver's seat back exactly where Rolf liked it. That was easy on this car, she thought, since there were presets for the radio and the driver's seat. She would just have to remember so Rolf would not find any reason to be short-tempered with her.

She took Pine Street west, driving the speed limit and gliding without braking through the timed signals. To get to Nob Hill and the Twin's Armoire she had taken Geary Boulevard to Masonic, swinging down to Bush Street and then cutting left to California Street on Larkin.

Agatha liked planning her routes around the city to take advantage of the timed lights on the wide one-way streets that San Francisco substituted for freeways.

She thought of the hideous freeways cutting into neighborhoods in other cities, bringing dust and darkness and smog, not to mention the constant roar of cars and trucks.

There was only one big freeway through San Francisco, a split aorta on the southeastern edge of the seven-mile-square city. It channeled the constant flow of traffic up from the Peninsula to the Bay Bridge and Interstate 80, and from there all the way to New York City.

She was glad the old cross-town elevated freeways had mostly been torn down after the earthquake in 1989. So much more sun and air now, she thought. So much quieter, and more people riding bicycles and walking.

This was like Europe; this was as it should be in a small city like San Francisco, where houses were built right next to each other, as they were in European cities.

Pine Street curved onto Masonic and Agatha turned right on Geary Boulevard. *Rolf will be in his home office downstairs*, she thought. She debated with herself about parking on the street; that way she wouldn't disturb him by opening the garage door. But he was very particular about parking the Mercedes in the garage. He kept the car spotless and always fretted when parking it in public locations.

"Some pig vill scratch it," he would say, growling the R in "scratch."

She wondered how she would manage to keep the dress money and get Rolf's permission to go shopping another day. In English the word was "wangle," she remembered. She would try to wangle a way to keep the money and go on a second outing. Wangle was a funny word that sounded like it must have been German to begin with. But then, English started out as mostly German originally, which made the similarity of the words not so odd.

She wanted to protect her rare outing for another day, but Rolf could very well change his mind and rescind his permission. She decided she would approach her request by making him fresh *spaetzle*. She would grate a little nutmeg into it the way he liked. With a fresh green salad and the chicken, she was confident the little noodles would put him in a cooperative mood.

Sometimes he told her that the Bavarian dishes she cooked were just like his beloved *Mutter*'s. Not often—he was a perfectionist about cooking—but *spaetzle* was so easy. Just flour and water and eggs and a little seasoning or cheese. She liked the way the dough gave under her hands as she kneaded it on the wide wooden cutting board.

Agatha loved her kitchen. That she loved it was a good thing, when she considered that Rolf insisted on her cooking everything fresh. He permitted no ordering in from any of the wonderful restaurants that crowded against each other in every neighborhood of San Francisco, and she was forbidden to buy pre-packaged or frozen food.

She enjoyed the process of making something from scratch. After all, she ate the delicious results along with Rolf. *God knows he lets me have everything I could want in the way of utensils and pans and knives*, she thought. Anything she asked for she could have, as long as she showed why a recipe called for it.

She had been daydreaming all the way out Geary Boulevard, and with a start she saw the Pacific Ocean and realized she'd arrived at 48th Avenue. She turned left and pulled up to the garage, pressing the door opener button that was built into the expensive car's electronic system.

Gliding in slowly, carefully, watching her

mirrors and taking care not to scrape against the narrow door jamb, she inched the gleaming car forward until the tennis ball suspended from the garage's ceiling touched the windshield. Rolf demanded precision in this as in everything, so she checked to be sure the tennis ball was not hanging crookedly. If it was, she would need to back up until the ball hung in a perfect plumb line. Before turning off the ignition, Agatha reset the radio and seat to Rolf's preferences.

Rolf had not come out of his office to watch her as she drove in. She wondered why not. He normally came out to supervise, to ensure nothing untoward had happened to his car.

It always made her nervous to have him watch, especially since he so rarely let her drive. She was used to taking the bus or walking, but today she was to have had heavy shopping bags and the bus wouldn't do. A taxi was out of the question; Rolf had thrown a fit the one time he saw her pull up to the house in a taxi. She had become ill in the grocery store, but Rolf declared that illness was no excuse for "throwing avay good money" and had docked the cost of the fare from her weekly expense stipend.

She climbed up the inside stairs from the garage into the upstairs hallway. Rolf had built his office at the garden end of the long narrow garage. Like most houses in San Francisco, the main living quarters were one level up from the street, above the ground-floor garage. Agatha's house was one of the few on the block with a third story as well, for the bedrooms.

She slipped off her shoes and stepped onto the white carpeting Rolf had insisted they install over the oak and mahogany hardwood floors. She preferred the warm glow of the wood, and promised him she would keep it waxed and shining, but he said it would only show scuff marks from shoes and besides, it was cold on his feet. *If he hates the cold so much,* she thought, *what is he doing living in San Francisco, where in August the wind and fog surging in off the cold Pacific forced you to dress like Admiral Peary to take a walk in Sutro Park across the street?*

Agatha hung her purse on its hook in the closet and put her lined raincoat onto its hanger. As she shut the closet door quietly, she heard a bump from upstairs. Looking up at the ceiling, she stood and waited and listened. She heard Rolf's voice, low and laughing, coming from their bedroom.

There was another bump, and she heard Rolf laugh again. She heard a second voice. A female voice. She recognized the laugh. It was that flashy one, that Linda, the big blonde who worked as his secretary, an administrator they called them now, in Rolf's real estate office down in Menlo Park.

Agatha stared at the ceiling. She listened to the two voices until she was certain that Rolf had sent her out shopping so he could bring that *dreckig hure*, that filthy bleached-blonde whore, into the house. Rolf had sent Agatha out shopping so he could *ficken* that *schweinisch nutte* here in the house, in Agatha's own bed, on the sheets she laundered and pressed through the old-fashioned mangle so they would be fresh and unwrinkled, exactly as he insisted they be.

She felt something in her midriff give way. Blood rushed to her face. She felt the heat of it, and waited for the heat to pass. When she was cool once more, she felt utter clarity about what she must do next. She stood up straight and took a deep breath.

"No more am I such a fool," she whispered.

With careful, silent footsteps she made her way back down the stairs to the garage. What she needed was in Rolf's office.

≈3≈

Asa blew out a deep sigh and slumped in his chair at Enrico's.

"Right now," he said, "it's not the gods who are helping me, it's you. Please, I don't know why I came here today, except now I think it was because you'd be here. I just need to talk through everything. If I can do that with someone who doesn't have a fixed opinion already, somebody who doesn't have any skin in the game, I think I'll be able to work my problems out. Or at least get started. Right now I am completely stuck."

"All right," I said, meeting his gaze. "We start at the beginning, then. But I want you to keep something in mind. These are just little colored pieces of paper, and I'm just a stranger saying whatever comes into my mind. It's your life, and your future, and you have control over what you say and do going forward. Is that understood?"

"Yes," he said. "Thank you."

I picked up the Crossing Card, the Emperor, to show him the Magician underneath it. "The Magician is a very complicated card, full of both contradictions and clarity, and it's where we start in your reading. Most of the time a card in this location of the layout is the key to you and your situation. Because all tarot readers rely on the intuition that reading cards trains in us, we use the book definitions of the cards only as guide-posts, but sometimes the book definition is the best place to begin.

"There are a zillion ways to interpret the cards, okay? Books and readers disagree all over the place. But this card is most often attributed to Mercury," I said. "He was called Hermes by the Greeks, and he was the messenger of the Gods. He was a god to the Egyptians as well. He's the adept, the master, the healer, the magus. He is also of dual natures, both male and female."

Asa's eyes jumped from looking at the card to looking up at me. He sat back in his chair and put his hands up to the sides of his head.

"What?" I asked him.

"Nothing. Tell me what else the Magician means," he said, leaning forward again and putting his hands down in his lap. I looked at him and waited.

Sometimes just waiting in silence will push the Querent to tell you what you need to know in order to proceed. Asa withstood the silence and my questioning look. He nodded down to the cards and back up to me, prompting me to continue. So I continued.

"The Magician also represents communication," I said, "both physical and psychic. On the table in front of him he has all the tools he needs to master his environment, and he uses his brilliance, his intelligence, his intuition, his intention, his will, to become an adept. Because of where he is in the layout, I think this card has a lot to say to and about you.

"One of the other common interpretations of this card is transformation," I said. "The Magician indicates talents or resources or tools you can or should use to fulfill your potential. You may need guidance or assistance to reach that potential, or you may be able to rely on your own judgment and intuition and skills.

"What do you do that is masterful?" I asked Asa. "That uses tools to create something brilliant and transformational? That's linked to the healing arts in some way? That involves relaying information back and forth quickly?"

I was speaking now from the part of me that doesn't consciously construct sentences.

"I started a company. We're doing research. It's very secret."

"Not government-secret though. It's about healing rather than weapons."

"It is," he said, a how-did-you-know-that look on his face. "And it will be a tremendous medical breakthrough. The venture capitalists have us all tied up with these draconian nondisclosure agreements so I can't tell you any more about it. But there are many more companies than ours working with the type of technology we're using."

"Who is 'us'?"

"A group of us started working together on this after we graduated from Stanford Medical School. There are other physicians and scientists on board now as well. Do you know what nanotechnology is?"

If you live in San Francisco, a short skip from the high-tech giants of Silicon Valley, you absorb techno-terminology by osmosis.

"Nano means billion. So I think you're working on something very small and very fast."

"Yes to both." He lowered his voice and looked over his shoulders to see who was nearby. The only other patron in the café was the big blond man sitting against the opposite wall, and he was paying no attention to us.

The wait staff at Enrico's are very civil to me when I read cards, and once they bring my tea they keep their distance unless I wave them over. It helps that my formal religious beliefs consist almost entirely in: 1) taking long walks on the beach; 2) being extremely pleasant to everyone in the world until they are rude to me or to anyone I am with at the time; and 3) prodigious over-tipping. Our waiter was standing next to the door to the inside section of the café. He could keep an eye on us but would not intrude.

Confident no one was listening, Asa turned back to me. "We're working on using nanorobots for organ reconstruction, and we're close to achieving some pretty amazing results. That's already more than I ought to tell you." He shrugged in apology.

"It sounds like science fiction," I said. "Nanorobots? How can anything possibly recreate a human organ?"

"That's the trillion-dollar question, isn't it? The thing is, nanotechnology means nothing more than working with extremely small things. A nanometer is about one hundred thousand times thinner than a sheet of paper. Since scientists began working in this field, everything from hand lotion to the coating on your sunglasses to pharmaceutical drug administration has been affected by advances in nanoscience. All that stuff cell phones can do now compared to just dialing a phone number with one of those big clunking handsets back in the late eighties? All of that is a result of nanotechnology."

Asa was caught up, enthusiastic, talking with his eloquent hands.

"The first major development in nanoscience that people generally know about was the electron microscope," he said. "The scientists who developed it figured out how to bombard whatever miniscule thing they wanted to look at, like a virus, with sub-atomic particles, and from how the bombardment reported its results to the computer, the computer was able to form an image of the thing that was being bombarded.

"What we've learned since then is that how you bombard things and what you bombard them with can change both entities in profound ways. A lot of the initial research in this field took place at Stanford, because of the linear accelerator they built. It's one the reasons I decided to go there for med school."

He stopped himself. "I'm sorry. I forget that not everybody gets as excited as I do about this topic."

"Well at least I get a glimmer of what you're excellent at, and the brilliant part is also pretty clear, because you know how to describe something very complicated so that I can almost believe I understand it."

I smiled. "Are you ready to look at the other cards here, and see what shape they take? No subatomic bombardment necessary."

Asa smiled back and nodded. I picked up the Emperor card. "I'm going to explain the tarot a little so you see why this reading is unusual, and why I had the initial reaction I did." I tapped the Emperor and Magician card against each other.

"There are twenty-two cards in the tarot deck that represent larger matters. Cycles in all human life, perhaps, or the universal processes we all go through. The twenty-two cards are called the Major Arcana, the big secrets, and they comprise about a fourth of the total deck.

"The rest of the tarot, the Minor Arcana, are the precursors to today's playing cards. There are four suits of fourteen cards each. Today we call the suits spades, hearts, diamonds, and clubs. The only Major Arcana card to make it into the modern card deck is the Fool, but now it's called the Joker.

"What took me by surprise when I saw your layout was the number of Major Arcana. On average we should see two or three out of the ten I put down. But here there are six of them.

"Why that matters is that when I see cards like this it usually means the Querent, meaning you, is in the middle of something that feels uncontrollable, unfathomable. So it doesn't surprise me that you feel stuck. What these cards say is that your only job right now is to survive and learn. Surf's up, dude, and your job is to stay on the board."

I smiled, and he looked up at me and nodded. He spread his arms and bent forward as if he were balancing on a tightrope. "Bitchen," he said.

"So let's see what we can glean from the information that's here, to keep you from wiping out. The Magician and the Emperor are both cards that deal with mastery. The Magician masters tools and communication to create an outcome; the Emperor masters himself and sets the boundaries of his realm. These two cards crossing like this create a sense of deep potential for greatness and achievement, because the Emperor organizes and structures his world so that the Magician can accomplish his will by using the right tools."

I looked up at Asa to see if he was with me, and he nodded at me to go on.

"But there is risk here as well," I said. "The Magician can act precipitously, rashly, and the Emperor can draw boundaries that are too narrow and that obstruct progress. He can be a control freak."

The next words I said simply came; I was allowing again rather than thinking.

"Sometimes the Emperor card represents someone else in your life, someone with power. The power can be financial or psychological, or maybe emotional? I have the impression there is someone, probably older and male, who has some measure of control over your creativity and the results you want to achieve. You've come up against this someone, and found him very compelling and controlling, and it's halted your progress, and you can't see your way past the obstacle yet.

"I know you've told me you're stuck," I went on, "and you mentioned the venture capitalists, but my impression is that you're stuck because of this one person or obstacle and because what you are doing is something this person, and I think it is a real person, does not want you to accomplish. I don't believe you are facing an internal obstacle. But whatever this obstacle is, you may not even be sure you should try to get around it. I think perhaps you have genuine respect for this person, and you wonder whether he may perhaps be right in trying to prevent you from completing your work."

I felt a shiver run up my back. Such a shiver is a sign to me that I have hit a target dead center. I was not physically cold; I was wearing jeans, running shoes with cotton socks, a long-sleeved T-shirt, a skinny crocheted scarf around my neck, and a leather jacket — the *de rigueur* layering required in San Francisco no matter what the season.

I lifted my eyebrows at Asa in a question, because he had closed his hands into fists and pressed them against his mouth. His cheeks had bloomed red and his dark eyes suddenly glittered with tears.

I waited for him. I've learned not to touch Querents during a reading, nor do I say anything until emotions wash through them and they are ready to continue. Asa's emotion would bring with it information we could work with, that would help him know what to do.

I had to wait a long time for him to recover himself. Six Major Arcana in the layout, only two down so far, and the four Minor Arcana were no walk in the park.

...*I will be the pattern of all patience; I will say nothing,* Shakespeare wrote for King Lear to say in the midst of a wild storm. So I sipped my cold tea. I watched the late morning traffic passing by. I wondered what there was in this dreadful storm of cards for me to learn. Because every reading I do for someone else teaches me something I need to know. What did I need to learn about transforming my life? About mastery of all the tools available to me? About healing?

I had no idea. So I said a little prayer for Asa. I threw in a little prayer for me, too.

≈4≈

Agatha stood still for almost a minute once she was in Rolf's office, making up her mind. She knew this was a big decision and she wanted to be certain she was ready to move ahead.

She realized she felt utterly clear, in the way any woman is clear when she has finished with a man and he will never win her back.

Agatha walked in her stockinged feet to Rolf's desk and pulled open the bottom left drawer, lifting out the key from the little cup hook that held it. She turned to the wall, unlocked the glass-fronted case, smelled the oil and metal, and took out what she needed.

She checked to be sure that what she had in her hand was ready and operational, locked the cabinet, tossed the key ring onto the empty desk surface, and tucked her hand behind her back.

She tiptoed slowly, soundlessly up the stairs to the third floor, to the master bedroom. She was glad for the carpeting now; it silenced her footsteps. The wooden banister smelled of lemon polish and the carpet of the lavender powder she sprinkled on it that left a sweet fragrance when she vacuumed.

Her thoughts shifted to the curtains she had sewn for the master bedroom, for all the bedrooms. She had trimmed the lampshades with ribbon to match the curtain fabric. She had sewn and embroidered the duvet cover for the down comforter. She had found extra-long fine percale sheets to go over the feather bed so it was like climbing into heaven at the end of each long, exhausting day. She had bought the perfect shaggy black sheepskin rug for the foot of the bed, so soft against her bare feet, and a black leather bench for Rolf to sit on while he pulled on his socks and shoes. The socks she had washed and matched; the shoes she had polished.

She had kept everything pristine, everything the way he demanded, everything just as he wanted it, with never an argument or complaint from her. No, complaints were his alone to register.

In the hallway she passed a mirror. She stopped to look at herself, the strong shoulders and square face, the light brown hair with gray in it now, the pale blue eyes with no makeup, the worry lines creasing her forehead. She looked her age, she knew. She was just a big farm girl in a clean cotton dress, so tall she had had to wear flat shoes when she married Rolf.

But farm girl or baroness, no woman deserved to be treated in such a disrespectful manner in her own home. She turned away from her reflection and tiptoed forward.

The bedroom door was slightly ajar, and she stood listening. They were not talking so much now. She could hear them moving around on the fresh sheets that were so smooth against one's skin. She pushed the door away from her slowly, and there they were, and now she smelled the musk of sex.

How odd people looked when they had sex. How comical they looked without clothing, with blemishes on their backsides and pouches of fat that they masked when dressed by wearing careful couture and strict undergarments. Rolf's flesh was such an unappealing color, really. And on Linda there was hair that didn't match from one place to another.

Linda was underneath, and she saw Agatha first: Agatha as still as a statue, Agatha's face odd, maybe even a little cheerful, Agatha's right hand hidden behind her back.

"Rolf," Linda said, moving her hand from Rolf's buttocks to his hip and tapping him with a long, French-manicured fingernail. "Your wife's here, hon."

Rolf turned his head and looked over his shoulder. He looked almost, thought Agatha, like a runner checking to see whether he was still ahead in the race and by how far.

His face was red as he rolled off Linda onto his back, and Agatha realized he was going to start shouting, that he would find a way to make this her fault. Agatha realized that an apology for *schtupping* his secretary in their marriage bed was not even remotely possible.

Sure enough, here it comes, Agatha thought. First the face reddens, then the deep breath, and finally the raised fist. He was like a two-year-old, really.

"Can you do nutting right?" he screamed. It was his typical approach to everything, she thought, to blame anyone but himself when something did not go according to his plan. Agatha smiled, and turned her head slightly, whether to deflect the sound or hear it more accurately she wasn't sure. She felt herself to be observing rather than evaluating.

Rolf looked at Linda and shook his head. "*Schatz*, you see? My vife is a *dumbkopf*," he said. "She cannot even correctly for a new dress go shopping." He threw a hand up in exasperation.

Linda snickered. "You have to admit it is a little funny," she said, between giggles.

Agatha noticed that Linda didn't seem the slightest bit embarrassed, lying there naked while her lover's wife stood there watching. Any normal person would be uncomfortable, but then Agatha saw that Linda had not pulled up the sheet to cover herself and her mismatched hair, her pouchy stomach. Agatha concluded that this affair must have been going on for a considerable time.

And then Rolf laughed too. The two of them, facing each other, laughing harder now, shaking their heads, leaning toward each other. Linda started to snort, like the pigs Agatha's father had raised on the family farm outside Lenngries, almost at the Austrian border.

"Go avay now," Rolf said, between laughs. "Now you see how it is going to be."

He put his hand on Linda's thigh and the two of them looked at Agatha boldly. "You are nutting to me now," he said, stern and commanding, his typical tone with Agatha for as long as she could remember.

"You vill cook and clean the vay you alvays haf," said Rolf, frowning as he did so often when speaking to Agatha. "To me dat is all you haf ever been good for. Now you go avay. You leaf us now." He lifted his hand off Linda's leg and shooed Agatha away.

Into Agatha's memory swept the many times over the years that she had tried to become pregnant, and then begged Rolf to consider adopting. Rolf blamed her and called her *unfruchtbar*, even though she knew from his mother that he had had mumps when he was fifteen and it was Rolf who was the problem. How many years now had she lived without anyone loving her?

"Vye are you still there standing?" he shouted. "Go avay at vunce! *Raus machen zie*! I vill get der dress money back from you ven vee are finished." He turned to Linda and shook his head.

"You see how it is," he said to Linda. "She is useless, only standing here, she does nutting but vat I tell her."

Agatha thought of the dress she would have bought, the dress Rolf thought she no longer deserved. She looked at the headboard, and the fabric that looked so perfect with the curtains. To make that headboard she had covered plywood with thick white batting, stretching the striped fabric carefully so the pattern was straight. She had pulled the buttons for the tufting through the plywood one by one, tying the shaggy twine off firmly, measuring and marking each spot exactly so the buttons would be evenly spaced and the stripes would line up perfectly.

She thought of how her hands had ached for two days afterward, from the chafing of the rough twine and the strain of pulling the trigger on the staple gun that fixed the fabric and batting firmly to the plywood.

Rolf's pistol would not be so difficult to fire as the staple gun, she thought, raising the gun and aiming at Rolf's upper torso. In the office she had checked that the gun was loaded and the safety off, and sure enough when she pulled the trigger the gun fired easily—much more easily than the staple gun. Wasn't that remarkable?

One, two. You could hardly miss at ten feet. One for him; one for her. It took only an instant. Then, to be sure, she walked a few steps forward and one, two again.

She looked around at the room. She remembered how she would have preferred soft, restful colors like rose and cream and sage, but Rolf wouldn't allow it; he said her preferences were too feminine. So the master bedroom colors were tans and grays, with black and scarlet for accents. Agatha had never found the decor restful. Dramatic and striking, yes, but not the serene retreat she could have relaxed in. Now, she realized, she could decorate the room any way she liked. She could decorate the entire house any way she liked.

The only thing I loved in this room was that headboard, she thought. *Oh well. I will go downtown to Britex for some new fabrics as soon as I put things in order here. There is always something lovely at Britex.*

≈5≈

Asa had settled himself. His eyes were still red, but he had stopped wiping away tears.

"Ready?" I asked.

"Yup."

"What was that?"

"A bunch of things," he said.

"What things?"

He took another moment to collect himself. "My dad. Sergei Abelev, the operations guy at our company. Marcus Blank, the chief venture capitalist. All of them. Any of them." He shrugged.

"Who stands out? Who came to mind first and brought the emotion with him?"

He sighed deeply. "My dad," he said at last, and looked at me, his eyes glittering again with tears. He swallowed and fought them back.

"Okay. We'll see where that takes us with the rest of these." I picked up the Nine of Swords.

"This is the foundation card. It has to do with root causes. It's the one you picked out earlier to comment on, which makes it important here." I handed the card to him. "I'd like you to tell me what comes to mind when you look at it. Don't edit or rule anything out. Just say whatever you think of."

He looked at the card for a moment. "People are making trouble. Maybe with malice. Somebody suspects threats or is making them. Everyone is unhappy. There could be a war but the swords and hands all seem lined up even though they're facing off against each other. Maybe the war is secret." He stopped and looked at me.

"Very astute, very perceptive. And because I want to work with your intuition as well as mine during this reading, let's agree that the groundwork for your situation was laid by a person or people who, at some time in your past, or perhaps throughout your life, have aligned themselves to create a serious problem for you, one that has caused you ongoing grief. Or it may be a problem you are not fully aware of yet."

"I'm aware of it."

"Maybe it is in fact your father, since he's the one who came to your mind first. If it is your Dad, then he may not have been in agreement with others who were involved, but ultimately everyone went ahead with whatever they did with or to you. Whatever that was, it ended up causing you heartache, and it continues to do so. My guess is it's the underlying motivation for your actions today."

"Damn," Asa said, shaking his head as if he should have realized something sooner. "Yes, that makes complete sense to me." He stared at the card.

Sometimes when I read cards I see images. I saw two white men and a white woman arguing in a white corridor. The woman wore a loose dress and had her hand on the taller man's arm. The other man wore a lab coat and glasses.

"Does your mother have red hair?" I asked Asa.

He sat back in his chair with a little thump. "Yes?"

"Is your father a good deal taller than she is?"

"Good Lord, how are you getting that from these cards?"

"I see a man and a woman arguing with another man in a corridor. A wide, white corridor with smooth gray floors and broad double doors at the end. Institutional-looking. From the way they all are dressed it seems to be a long time ago. Your mother doesn't agree with your father about something, but she's losing the argument."

"She did lose." Asa crossed his arms, hugging himself, and shook his head. "I can't talk about this. Not yet. Can we keep going, even if I don't tell you everything?"

"Sure. Of course. This is a tough set of cards. You tell me whatever you feel comfortable with and we'll leave it at that. Let's look at the High Priestess, shall we? She's the influence that is just passing."

I took over more strongly now, my intuition telling me I had to make the reading easier on Asa, that he needed to disengage emotionally in order to get through this.

"The High Priestess, like all the Major Arcana, can mean many things. She is about potential, study, solitude, devotion, tenacity, the promise of fruitfulness. I'd say most of your time recently has been spent with your nose to the grindstone. You tell me you're close to a breakthrough, and that would make sense with this card. I think you have been applying everything you know to a problem, and my take on it is that you will achieve the result you want. The caution is that it may not bring you what you hoped it would."

"Why not?"

"Because of the Crowning card," I said, pointing at Death.

"Does that mean I'm going to die?"

"Nothing like that."

But of course it can mean death. I couldn't tell Asa that. No ethical reader will tell a Querent that the Death card means a Querent's literal death.

But in Asa's layout Death was followed by the Ten of Swords, "Ruin," and the two in combination are downright terrifying. I did think someone was going to die, not that I would ever admit that to Asa.

Tarot cards are just colored pieces of paper, and I'm just a woman in a café.

"The Death card can mean death," I began carefully, "but only rarely. It usually refers—almost always refers—to massive life change. The alteration of circumstances, station, personhood, belief system, connections; it is a complete turnaround in some essential element of the individual. Our bodies change all our cells every seven years or so. We are literally reborn over and over again in our lifetimes. So the Death card most often represents that sort of ongoing renewal.

"The most prominent factor in your situation at this moment," I continued, "is also your crowning goal. Your hope is to make such an indelible change in your life that it's as if you or a part of you will be reborn.

"It's not something to be afraid of," I went on. "It's extremely difficult to pass through, but that's what life does to us. Life forces us to make major changes. Physically, puberty is an example of a life change that would warrant this card in a reading. Its location in the layout means your deepest hope is to undergo this kind of change."

Asa was ashen, gaping at me.

"What are you thinking?" I asked softly.

"Nothing," he said, shaking his head and clearing his throat. "Nothing I can talk about, anyway. Keep going, please?" He stared down at the cards, fists curled up to his mouth again, his arms pressed together on the tabletop.

"The Ten of Swords is soon to come," I said. I was careful about my language here, marshalling my tact but trying not to filter or control the meaning.

"It's called Ruin in some decks. I think something you have set in motion is at risk. It may fall apart, and in an unpleasant way. Something about your world is—there's the possibility of something shattering."

The word was out of my mouth before I could soften it.

"Do you know what will shatter?" he asked.

"I don't." I saw an image of Asa, but it wasn't him either. It was a young woman, very like him but clearly female. Tallish, slender, short dark hair, the same bright black eyes. I held off asking about her. I didn't want Asa to associate her with the Ruin card.

I needed time to think of a way to protect her, and Asa too, if I wasn't mistaken. The woman I was seeing in my mind's eye had to be Asa's sister, and my little colored pieces of paper were telling me that some of the threat these cards foretold was headed her way.

≈ᕼ≈

Agatha realized that Linda and Rolf were both leaking; the mattress would be ruined. It was likely she would have to start over altogether on the headboard. Depending on how the bullets had traveled, she might have to replace the box spring and even some of the wall plaster. She needed to move swiftly.

She found it energizing to have a clear purpose.

She went to the closet and put on her old slippers to go back down to the garage, where she found the heavy plastic tarp with which Rolf would drape the car when he did his woodworking. Back in the bedroom, she heaved the leather bench out of the way and spread the tarp on the floor at the foot of the bed.

Grabbing Rolf by the feet, she dragged him

toward her until he thudded onto the tarp. He was heavy and her slippered feet slid a little on the plastic, but she was used to lifting heavy grocery bags every day, and her cast-iron cookware was heavy too. When she was a girl she had helped her father slaughter the pigs. She was a big farm girl. She was strong enough for this work.

Touching Linda was unpleasant. Her skin was warm and spongy. Agatha told herself it would only take a moment, that it was necessary, and hauled Linda toward the tarp until she fell onto Rolf.

"Your turn to be on top," Agatha heard herself muttering. She pulled the corners of the tarp together and tied them with a plastic garbage bag tie. "Like a big *bouquet garni*," she giggled, and then checked herself; she was shaking a little now and thought perhaps adrenaline was pushing her a tiny bit out of control. She took a deep breath and let it out slowly to calm herself. The room smelled of the gunshots. She lifted the windows open to air things out.

Gripping the tarp, she began to pull. "This is not so hard," she thought as the plastic slid over the carpeting.

She was headed for the guest bathroom. The master bedroom doorway was a tight squeeze for a moment, but she managed to heave the unruly lumps toward the tarp's center and pull it through without tearing the plastic.

She kept an eye out over one shoulder as she backed up, then looked forward again, checking the hall carpet to see if anything was escaping. The rug looked fine so far. There was always the carpet steamer in the garage in case the rug became stained.

At the guest bathroom she had to make another adjustment to get the tarp through the doorway, and then there they were, safely tucked up and tidied away where she could attend to them later.

First things first. Over the years she had learned to be organized and methodical, traits she realized were going to prove very useful during the coming days. She headed down to the kitchen.

She sat at the island with a fresh cup of coffee and a pad of paper, making a list with her favorite fine-point pen. Four minutes later she checked to see if she had forgotten anything:

- Bedding
- Mattress
- Bullets
- Box spring?
- Call R's office
- Headboard?
- Plaster?
- R & L bag/bury
- Bank
- Paint?

- Fabric
- Pistol
- Linda clothing/car?

She left room on the page for any additions she might add later; after all, she had never made a list like this before. It was probable she would need to make amendments as she checked things off, but the list looked to Agatha like a solid start.

All right: the mattress and bedding first. Back upstairs she climbed with a selection of Rolf's woodworking tools and a full box of dark green garbage bags.

Pulling on a pair of yellow latex housekeeping gloves, she stripped off the bedding and stuffed it into two bags, tying them shut. She threw the bags down the first flight of stairs, walked down after them, and threw them down the second flight to the washing machine in the garage. She started the sheets and mattress pad in cold water with plenty of bleach. She knew, as every woman knew, that hot water would set the bloodstains.

She would throw away the bedding later, but the stains had to be washed out first. The feather bed she would discard and replace after she mended and hand-scrubbed it in the deep sink, since the feathers could not go in the washing machine. She put the garbage bag holding the feather bed in her sewing room for the time being.

Downstairs at Rolf's workbench again she unboxed his high-powered portable jigsaw, the one he had bought to make ornate moldings and fretwork for the cuckoo clocks he designed and built as a hobby. Back up in the master bedroom the jigsaw vibrated in her hand. She grabbed the elastic mattress handle and pulled hard to shift the queen-sized mattress off the edge of the box spring. She began to slice at the mattress, putting the severed chunks into garbage bags and tying the bags shut as she filled them up.

It was hard work, and she had to stop to let the jigsaw cool down more than once. It took almost an hour to cut up and bag the mattress, and when Agatha shut off the jigsaw for the last time she sat down to rest on the leather bench where she had pushed it against the wall.

She looked around her at the accumulated garbage bags. It struck her that, puckered and tied at the top, the garbage bags looked like huge seaweed-covered Chinese dumplings. She felt the hysterical giggle threaten to start. She swallowed hard and forced herself to think. Should she check the list in the kitchen?

No, she had to rest a little for now. In the mattress she had found two of the bullets, and she had rinsed and placed them in Rolf's coin tray until later. The bullets were on her list, so she wouldn't forget them. She could see no damage to the box spring, nor could she see any blood on it, which made the clean-up so much easier. The pillows were ruined, but pillows were easy to replace, and she was happy to see that the head-board was intact. She could recover it with any fabric she liked and it would be as good as new.

The undamaged headboard meant the wall plaster was also undamaged. The other bullets must still be in Rolf and Linda, she concluded.

She was pleased that she could cross two po-tential tasks off her list. What a time savings that would be! She would have to vacuum up the little fluffs of mattress foam that had flown away from the jigsaw and settled on the rug, though; vacu-uming would have to be added to the list.

Agatha found herself shaking; she realized she was sweating and cold at the same time. She put on her thick beige wool household cardigan and went downstairs to the kitchen. She poured herself a glass of cold water from the filter pitcher in the refrigerator and took a long drink. She sat down to update her list.

"Vacuuming," she added. She did not cross out any tasks yet. Not until the mattress garbage bags were disposed of and a new mattress in-stalled on the bed could she consider the mattress task completed.

From under the sink she brought out a house-keeping scarf and an apron. She had forgotten to put those on before she started, and now the nice dress she had worn shopping would have to go to the cleaners to remove the sweat stains.

"Wait," she thought. "Of course not. I must

wash it and then throw it away. It will have to go."

She was sorry about having to lose the dress. Agatha had never thought the day would come when she would thank Monica Lewinsky for setting an example by shoving that incriminating dress into her closet instead of throwing it away. It was indeed a funny world.

Agatha felt refreshed by the cool drink of water and ready to go back to work. She left the empty glass sitting out on the countertop; she shuddered briefly at the disorder of it, the dirty glass sitting there where anyone could see it rather than tucked away promptly where it belonged, on the upper rack of the dishwasher.

She wondered whether she could ever go to bed and sleep soundly with any sort of mess sitting out overnight in the house. It had never been a possibility before now.

Halfway up the stairs, she heard the doorbell. No one ever rang the doorbell except the Jehovah's Witnesses. They were immune to discouragement or were perhaps illiterate; Rolf had placed a large "No Soliciting" plaque right above the doorbell button. But if the Jehovah's Witnesses were illiterate, Agatha wondered, how could they read *The Watchtower*?

She bent down to peek through the glass of the demi-lune transom window over the front door.

Parked at the curb in front of her house was a black and white San Francisco police car.

The doorbell rang again.

Agatha sat down with a thump on the stair step and gripped the newel post. She stared at the front door and held her breath.

The policeman knocked now, hard and loud.

"Mrs. Hein?" he called in a very authoritative voice, like Rolf's voice. "San Francisco Police."

≈7≈

I was worried about Asa now. His color was not good; his face was green around the edges, like he was about to hurl.

"Are you okay?" I asked him. "Do you want to keep going? Would you like some water or anything?"

"I'm fine," he said. "Please don't stop. I need to hear this. I'm fine." He leaned forward and sat up in his chair. "I'm fine," he repeated. His skin's green tinge faded to a pallor that looked slightly less queasy.

"What's this card mean?" he asked, pointing at the Five of Wands.

"That's the outcome. We'll get to that one

soon. The next card is this one." I pointed to the Tower.

"This position in the layout represents what you fear," I said, "or sometimes readers call it the answer in the layout. I think it's possible to reconcile the two ideas, since often what we fear most has a way of showing up time and time again for us to deal with. What we fear most can be intended to lead us to answers about ourselves that free us to be more courageous in how we live.

"The Tower is the card of sudden, rude awakenings. Think of the Tower of Babel, built by men who deluded themselves that they could reach God by building a tower. God struck the tower down for their arrogance, and made them all speak different languages so they couldn't understand each other. The card here means some sort of overdue comeuppance for you.

"One of these days, and reasonably soon, you'll smack yourself on the forehead and realize you've been a dunce. There won't be any doubt about it. You'll know right away that whatever it is you've just figured out about yourself or your behavior relates to this card. You'll know because you'll feel chagrin, and probably remorse, and you'll know you need to make something right with someone close to you whom you've mistreated or ignored in some crucial way. It's no fun, this card. And it's in the fear position here, which means you may try to fight off the realization for longer than you should. Or it can mean you already suspect what you've done that was so misguided, and you've been refusing to face it."

"Does it say who it is I've mistreated? Who the person is I've got to apologize to?"

I waited for my intuition. No intuitions spoke up.

"Anyone. Everyone," I said. "Assume it's anyone and everyone."

"Can I just throw a please-forgive-me party?" He was laughing. "Get it over with in one shot, with catered hors d'oeuvres and an open bar?"

We smiled at each other. For now Asa was doing okay. Keep going.

"The next card is others' opinions, the support and assistance you can expect from those close to you. It's the Hermit, and he's reversed, meaning upside down. A reversed card means something different than when it's right-side up, but the potential for the original meaning is still in there.

"The Hermit can mean sagacity, wisdom, truth. He's considered the third magus in the deck, along with the Magician and the Hierophant. He holds up a lamp to light the way for himself, and it's the lamp of his learning and intelligence and goodness.

"Reversed, there is often something impetuous, heedless, unrehearsed about what others are saying and doing. They are not being wise or good. Your family and friends and co-workers are afraid, overly cautious, maybe hiding things from you. And some may even be plotting." I stopped myself. There was more to it than that, but I had said enough for now. No freaking out the Querent any more than he already was.

"The Seven of Pentacles is the defining card." I was moving quickly through the last two cards. Everything in me said this reading needed to be over with fast.

"Some call this location in the layout the hope card. This card implies dissatisfaction with your progress to date. Perhaps you have money worries after putting in so much time and effort with not much pay. Perhaps the results aren't as fruitful as you wish. This card says you want to stop and take stock of how much more work and how many more resources or funds it will take to get the results you want, and whether it's all worth it. Because you're doing something no one has ever done, there's no predicting how long it will take to do it, or what frustrations and delays you'll encounter along the way."

Asa nodded his head. "That is entirely true, that one," he said, pointing at the card. "Today I made a list of the time I've put into this project, how many hours a day, and how many meetings I've had to attend to make the case for more funding. Everybody gets pissed off when we hit yet another unanticipated setback, but if anybody already knew how to do this, we wouldn't be pursuing it."

He went on, tapping the card on the table as he ticked off the items on his list. "I've lost track of my friends. I've had fights with my family. I can't even guess how much weight I've lost from forgetting to eat when I've been working in the lab late at night. I really believe it will be worth it in the long run, but right now work doesn't feel like much fun. Especially since our progress has been slower than everyone had expected."

He put the card back in place. "This morning's checklist is why I took the day off and drove up here. I just needed to get away from everything and think about what I want to do instead of what I feel like I have to do." He sat back, nodding his head. This was a good sign, I knew from experience. He was feeling a mounting sense of release from whatever had him ensnared.

"The last card, the outcome or ending, is the Five of Wands," I said. "Wands are attributed to inspiration and energy, and fives are the fulcrum—the midpoint from one to ten in the suit—and they represent change or transition.

"The Five of Wands often means competition, sometimes rather fierce. You'll have to stand up for what you want to do, and probably in the face of some difficult challenges from the people closest to you."

I paused. "You have a sister."

"How the hell do you know that?" Astonishment showed on his face.

"She looks just like you. Listen, you need to look out for her. Keep your eye on her. She's not your enemy here, okay? To me, she seems to be the only one on your side in this whole thing."

"Yes," Asa agreed, "that's true. She is." We were looking at each other now, not the cards.

"What's her name?"

"Beth."

"Do everything you can think of to keep her safe." I didn't know how to make my dread on her behalf any clearer to Asa without being more specific about the proximity of her image in my mind to the Death card and the Ten of Swords.

"I promise," he raised a hand to swear.

"The key for you is to sustain your inspiration. Keep it foremost. Don't lose sight of what started this whole thing going. Inspiration lit up the pathway through the forest for you at the outset, and inspiration is what brought you here to this place when things became too difficult to figure out. When you find yourself at a loss, ask yourself 'what do I really want?' and listen for what comes to mind first. Let that inner voice guide you."

I was quiet. I watched as Asa picked up the Death card and stared at it for a few seconds. Then he picked up the Tower.

I waited until he put them both down and

looked up at me. I raised my eyebrows in a question and he nodded.

I gathered up the cards and shuffled them loosely, setting them down on the scarf beside me.

"How are you doing?" I asked him.

He put his thumb and forefinger to his chin and frowned in mock thoughtfulness.

"Hmmmm. Well, first, thank you so much. You really have helped me. I think you know that, though."

"The oracle knows all."

"But the oracle doesn't tell all."

"Neither does the Querent."

"Fair enough." Asa thought for a moment. "I have one more question."

"By all means." I held out the cards to him.

"I don't think the cards can help me with this."

"What is it then?" I put the cards back down on the silk.

"Do you know any bodyguards? Like Secret Service types?"

I was surprised and then again I suppose I wasn't all that surprised. Not after the cards I had just seen.

"I know the ideal fellow," I said. "Just the man for the job."

"How can I get in touch with him?"

I pointed over Asa's shoulder to the big blond

man sitting alone against the opposite wall of the café.

"He's sitting right over there."

≈*8*≈

Agatha couldn't decide whether to open the front door or not. When the policeman knocked again, she heard in the knock more commitment and determination than experimentation, and she decided it would be better to open the door than continue to ignore it. This police officer acted as if he knew someone was home and he was not going to give up without a response.

Because of Rolf's variable moods, she was practiced at reading a man's intentions from his slightest actions and speech. She focused her attention on reading this policeman as she let go of the newel post and walked downstairs.

"Who is it?" she asked through the door.

"San Francisco Police, ma'am. We had a report of gunshots. Open the door please." It was not a request.

Agatha put on the chain and opened the door. She stuffed her gloves in her apron pocket, putting her hand up to her headscarf and tucking loose hairs into it.

"What did you say?" she asked.

The policeman was six feet tall at least, with buzzed short hair and big shoulders. A black radio transmitter perched next to his collar like a charred bird. He was wearing a long-sleeved shirt with a yellow SFPD patch on the bicep. His thumbs rested on his woven black leather belt, which was crowded with holster and gun, flashlight, baton, taser, battery pack. Agatha wondered how he could remember where to reach if he needed something in a hurry. She supposed policemen must practice.

"Did you not hear me knocking, ma'am?"

"I'm sorry. I was vacuuming."

"Your neighbor reported hearing gunshots. She said they came from your house. You are Mrs. Hein, are you not? Is everything all right here?"

"Good heavens yes. I'm Mrs. Hein, and I've just been doing housework. The vacuuming and the laundry."

She gripped the doorknob on her side of the door so her hand would stop shaking. She saw the policeman looking at her nice dress under her apron and sweater. She thought he might be wondering who would wear a dress to do vacuuming and laundry.

"Mrs. Partierre is always worried about everything," Agatha said, waving her free hand dismissively toward the house next door and then tucking her hand into a fist and sliding it into her apron pocket. Was there blood on her hand? She didn't dare look.

"Mrs. Partierre is forever hearing burglars and calling all the neighbors." Agatha added a note of aggravation to her voice. "And with the traffic on Geary Street there is always backfiring."

The officer looked at her closely. He is assessing if I am nervous or not, Agatha decided. She held herself still and looked back at him steadily.

"Is there anyone here with you in the house?" he asked.

"I do not think my husband would say it was wise of me to answer a question like that," she said firmly, "but because you are a policeman I will tell you I am the only one at home. My husband is at his work."

"And you didn't hear any gunshots." It was a statement rather than a question.

"No, I did not. But with the vacuum on that is all I hear." Agatha smiled and shrugged.

Upstairs a phone rang. It was Rolf's cell phone. Agatha gazed up the stairs.

"Well, I'll let you get that. Thank you for your time, Mrs. Hein," the policeman said. "Take care." He was turning to go. *Please you will keep going*, Agatha prayed.

"Goodbye now," she called to him as he walked down the front steps to his patrol car. She shut the door and leaned to rest her forehead against the dark wood.

I nearly asked him if he would like some coffee, she thought, and a laugh choked her for a moment. She went upstairs to power off Rolf's cell phone.

She went to the kitchen and poured another cool glass of water. Checking her list, she lifted the phone and called Rolf's Menlo Park office. Betsy the receptionist answered, and Agatha asked Betsy if she had been told that Rolf was going to spend the next few days calling on high-tech corporate prospects in Massachusetts. She crossed "Call R office" off the list as she spoke.

"Do you know where Mr. Hein can be reached?" Betsy asked her. "I've had a call from a client because Mr. Hein isn't answering his cell phone."

"I have no idea. Linda called and gave me the message so that I would not cook his dinner." Agatha felt confident that this was the right information to offer.

"Oh, well, then I'll check with her," Betsy said abruptly. "Thank you, Mrs. Hein. You have a nice day now."

Agatha hung up the phone. *"Mein Gott*, everyone in his office knows what I am just now discovering," she said aloud, and walked to the dining room to get the electric carving knife that Rolf loved to use on the Christmas goose, "because it is efficient," he said. Just to be safe, to avoid another trip down and up the stairs, she picked up the cleaver from the knife block.

It was time for the next item on her list.

≈9≈

"Of course you know a guy," Asa laughed at me and turned around to look behind him. "Who is he?"

"His name is Thorne Ardall."

I lifted my hand slightly, palm open in a casual "hello" sign. Thorne didn't appear to be watching us, but he stood up. He kept standing up for some time before he was fully upright, heading over to our table. He started out ten yards away and he covered the distance, without hurrying or even moving his legs all that noticeably, in no time flat.

Once at Marine World a uniformed man walked past me holding a full-grown Bengal tiger on a thin leather leash. I had heard the keeper's approaching footsteps behind me because there had been a sudden hush amidst the noise of the crowd, but I had not heard any sound that indicated a tiger was passing right next to me.

The tiger was eight feet long from his nose to the base of his spine, and then there was his tail. He was as tall as my hips and he was less than two feet away from me as he passed by, stepping noiselessly on paws the diameter of salad plates. His walk was sinuous and utterly silent. The keeper was fast-walking to match the humongous cat's unhurried pace.

Everyone who saw the tiger melted backwards away from him, away from the path they saw him taking. Children did not ask if they could pet him; they closed their eyes and hid behind their Dads' legs and peeked out to see the six-hundred-pound marvel go by.

Watching Thorne approaching our table reminded me of seeing that tiger. You can't hear Thorne walking, his movement through the tables was sinuously feline, and people tend to step backwards when they see him.

He was wearing a green oxford cloth button-down shirt and black jeans. The shirt lit up the yellow and brown flecks in his deep-set green eyes. He was smooth-shaven and his skin was bronzed from sunshine.

"You rang?" he said to me, and then gazed down at Asa.

Asa stood up to introduce himself, throwing

his shoulders back in a vain attempt not to look miniscule next to six feet eight inches and two hundred sixty pounds.

Asa's hand disappeared inside Thorne's, except for a slender thumb peeking out. "I'm Asa Ballantine." He didn't squeak like Alfalfa saying hello to Darla, but I think it took some effort not to.

"Thorne Ardall."

"Sit, please," I said. "Asa wants to ask you about what you do."

Asa sat down. Thorne pulled out a chair and lowered himself slowly onto it, tensing as he settled in case the chair collapsed. It was like watching a helicopter attempt a landing on a card table.

Thorne seated himself next to me against the wall, where there was nothing behind him and he could see everything ahead and to the sides of him. His mop of blond hair fell over his forehead. I could smell the vetiver-scented soap he used.

From under the unruly blond thatch he was observing and assessing Asa. I knew he would miss nothing about Asa's appearance or demeanor. From this examination he would probably guess what kind of car Asa drove and what his favorite breakfast cereal was.

I sat silently, the pattern of all patience.

"Xana tells me you are in the business of bodyguarding," Asa said.

"Yes. In current parlance it is referred to as

'personal security,' but call it what you like."

That was quite a long statement for Thorne. Asa was a new client and Thorne apparently didn't want to scare him with awesome tiger-like taciturnity.

"What might the security involve? I don't know much about it."

Asa's candor was a pleasant surprise. A lot of people meet Thorne and immediately try to impress him with various forms of bullshit; sometimes they float information off-handedly about their wealth, or make spurious claims of knowledge about bodyguards and weaponry, or sometimes they'll try to intimidate him with assertions of political power.

Thorne tolerates the bullshit for maybe thirty seconds, sometimes less. He doesn't respond other than to stand up and walk away. Sometimes they yell things at him as he disappears. If their words were physical things they would bounce like ping pong balls off a steel backboard.

"I ensure your safety," he said.

Asa took that in. "What do I need to know about you? And what do you need to know about me?"

Once again I was surprised. Most people ask Thorne for references or a resumé, both utterly futile requests. Thorne either prompts instantaneous and complete trust, which means to Thorne that the potential employer is trustworthy, or he prompts instantaneous suspicion, which means, to Thorne anyway, that the potential employer is a crook. Thorne explained this to me when I asked about his selection process. He does not care to work for doubting crooked employers.

"I do everything that needs to be done, and you rely on me completely," Thorne said. "You pay me in cash and I do not appear on employment records, check registers, tax returns, or other physical or electronic documentation."

Asa tilted his head and looked at Thorne, at the steady gaze of the hooded green-brown eyes with the yellow flecks, and then glanced at me. I tilted my head in inch to the right, grinned, and waggled my eyebrows. Sometimes the Groucho thing proves helpful when newbies are dealing with Thorne.

"We usually pay vendors by direct deposit or electronic funds transfer," Asa said.

"I have no bank account. No e-mail. No phone listing."

"I don't mean to be difficult, but how can that be?"

"I am invisible," Thorne said.

Asa laughed. "Not hardly."

"Off the grid then."

Asa just shook his head. I think he realized just how incredibly difficult it is to be off the grid nowadays.

"And do you two work together?" Asa asked.

Thorne looked at me to field that one.

"We have a working relationship, yes," I said.

I have found that this way of characterizing how Thorne and I are connected seems to raise the fewest questions. Calling him my tenant triggers inquiries about why we are so often together.

We are not physical lovers, not at this point anyway. I am not accepting wagers on future developments, nor, given my pitiful track record in romantic pursuits, am I anxious to push ahead to the next level, as it is now called.

He and I met when Thorne drove his car into my house one foggy night, and against any sane person's better judgment I took him in and doctored his bullet wound. We tracked down the killer who had shot him, but from the moment I let him into my house the two of us formed a partnership for which the precise term does not seem to have been coined.

Thorne lives in an apartment on the ground floor of my house and I live upstairs. There is a locked door between the floors, not that such a thing would stop Thorne if he didn't feel like cooperating. We both appear to like the arrangement just fine, thanks, and, oh yes, please mind your own damned business.

My mother, Louisa Duncan Livingston Monaghan Bard of Darien, Connecticut, thinks it is nice that I have a man available for those household chores a woman ought not to be required to do.

"Men should do the vacuuming," she announced. "They have the upper body strength."

Mater—what my four siblings and I call her but never to her face—also asserted that installing a tenant was a smart fiscal decision. Which it would be, if Thorne paid any rent. Instead he bought a big BMW and registered it in my name.

He has money, in the form of gold coins he buys with the cash he is paid for personal security. He sells the coins when he needs more cash than he has on hand. He feels comfortable carrying a lot of cash around. Even the boldest thieves step backward from a tiger.

My mother has not met Thorne. He clears out when I inform him of an impending visit from Mater. "I can handle you," he once said to me when I asked him why, "and I can handle your mother. I can't handle you when you are around your mother."

Asa had been quiet for a minute, no doubt thinking about the weirdness of somebody who never received spam, had no ATM card, and had never filed a tax return.

"How long have you two known each other?"

"Long enough," I said. "But that isn't the basis for your decision. Listen to your inner voice and decide. Do you trust him?"

Asa thought about that. After a few seconds he turned to Thorne.

"When can you start?"

"When I sat down." Thorne smiled his minimal smile.

Asa reached and the two men shook hands again.

"Well, then, you two will need to work out the details." I rolled my cards into their silk scarves.

"Wait," said Asa. "You asked me to provide you with something of value, to balance out the reading."

"You just did." I nodded at Thorne.

"I'll think of you with good thoughts," I said to Asa, "and don't forget what I said about your sister."

"Sister?" Thorne looked at me. I nodded my head.

"I'll need helpers," Thorne said to Asa. "You can pay them or I can."

"Whatever you need," Asa said.

He turned to face me. "I'd like to hug you, if you'll allow it." I allowed it. He put his arms around my shoulders and, as some people will do, rubbed one hand up and down on my shoulders. A sincere hug, no creepiness, just gratitude.

"Thank you so much," he whispered.

"You are very welcome."

I pulled back, looking him in the eyes. Asa smiled and I smiled back. He sat down again.

"Tell me what I need to do," he said to Thorne.

I tucked my cards into my bag, waved goodbye at Thorne, and headed over to find the waiter, Marco, who immediately stepped through the door of the café to the outside terrace. I gave him fifty dollars for my peppermint tea and his benign neglect. Marco and I were accustomed to this exchange.

"See you next time, Miss Bard. Thanks again and have a good day," Marco said.

Thorne and I don't have to say a lot in order to be understood by each other. Our tacit rapport is a very pleasant plus. We don't touch each other in public. Or private, for that matter.

Thorne doesn't like hugging people hello or goodbye. He likes to keep his sight lines open, is my guess, although I believe Shaquille O'Neal is the only one who could block his sight line.

I don't ask Thorne about his physical reticence. I don't really require an explanation. It's just one of those things about Thorne, take it or leave it.

I walked out to the sidewalk. Thorne wasn't looking at me but he saw me. He sees everything.

≈*10*≈

Agatha had made a neat job of it. Everything was tightly bagged and sealed with tape, nothing too heavy for her to carry, all twenty bags shifted down to the garage and settled carefully against the unpainted drywall outside Rolf's office.

At the end of the south wall closest to the garage door were the ten bags holding the mattress and washed bedding; at the other end of the wall, closest to Rolf's office, were the twenty bags holding Rolf and Linda. In the bagging process she had retrieved the other two bullets, washed them, and put them with the others in Rolf's coin dish on his dresser. She had picked up the casings from the bullets and placed them in the same dish.

She returned upstairs and vacuumed the bedroom thoroughly, back and forth twice over the entire area, hoovering up all the mattress fluff. She used the attachment to reach under the bed frame and suck up the little escapees, and made a final search using a flashlight she kept in the nightstand. In the flashlight's beam she spotted and vacuumed up a lurking, incriminating foam puff stained with bloody mattress filling. She was glad she had been so careful.

She lifted the full vacuum bag out of the machine and dropped it into a garbage bag, along with the cleaver and electric knife, both of which she had washed carefully and taped into a bubble wrap cocoon.

She rolled up the wide pink heavy floor paper she had laid down as protection on the carpeting. Rolf had purchased and used the roll of floor paper to protect the carpets when the painters were in the house two months ago. She carried the crumpled paper down to the living room fireplace. Spotting the roll of leftover paper in the garage was serendipity; tonight it would make a cheerful fire after the fog rolled in and the living room grew chilly.

What next? She checked her list. Time to rinse the plastic tarpaulin. In the guest bathroom she gathered the tarp up by the corners and lifted it into the tub, then stripped off her clothes and climbed in with it. She turned on the shower. She needed to freshen up, and it was easier to handle the unwieldy, and quite soiled, plastic by holding it up in sections to the hand-held wand sprayer. She would have to throw it away, but only when it was glisteningly clean.

The tarp had been very useful, draped completely across all the bathroom fixtures while she worked. She had been careful to keep everything contained, counting out and opening all the garbage bags she would need right at the start, being extra careful not to leave any traces around the tops as she loaded them up.

Pick the garbage up with one gloved hand, hold the prepared bag open with the other, drop the garbage into the bag, tie the bag shut. Such a simple routine, really. It had gone like clockwork, like one of Rolf's cuckoo clocks.

She felt clean now. Warm and pink and refreshed. She hung up the wand sprayer, left the plastic sheet to drain in the tub, and stepped out onto the fluffy green mat. Her dress, sweater, slippers, underwear, scarf and apron were bunched in the sink. Wash them and give them to Goodwill, she thought, wrapping a towel into a turban around her wet hair.

She pulled a wide green bath towel around her and walked to her bedroom. No one had ever used these green towels before. No one had ever stayed in the guest room. That would change now that the house was hers. She would renew her friendships. She would invite overnight visitors. This would be a house full of laughter and good food and enjoyment. She would fill vases with beautiful roses from her garden.

Would the house ever be filled with love? She wondered. She remembered when Rolf had first courted her, when she was still young and unfamiliar with the way men could treat women. She knew now that he was attentive to her then only because he was interested in acquiring her father's farm, and that he saw her, an only child, as the first step on his way to amassing wealth by owning and selling land and buildings. As soon as her father died, Rolf had sold the farm and they had moved to America, where her indentured servitude had begun.

Agatha halted her daydreaming; she realized that love in her future might be too much to hope for. For now there was work to do.

Dressed in sensible tan slacks and a brown cotton pullover Rolf had given her that she had never cared for and wouldn't mind discarding once all her work was done, Agatha returned to the kitchen to see where things stood on her list.

She couldn't decide whether it would be wise to go to the bank right away. Would the police check things like that when the time came? She decided she had better do it right away, and if anyone questioned her later she would say that Rolf had arranged for her to have access to funds in his absence. He kept the personal bank account information in his office downstairs. She couldn't think what to do about the real estate business for the time being. That would have to wait.

She went down to the office. She decided to start with the desk, and then see what was in the credenza and file cabinet. She began pulling open desk drawers. She had never been permitted to do more than dust and polish and vacuum in this room; she felt a nervous thrill as she poked around to see what Rolf had kept private from her. She spotted a ring of keys in a little tray in the center drawer of the desk, and it was a simple matter to try them and find the correct one for the credenza.

She found a full-page-sized checkbook, with three perforated checks on each page and the register information on a tear-off stub at the left edge of each check. There were three other checkbooks in the credenza as well.

Using another key, she opened the file cabinet and found the statements for each bank account in the top drawer. There were four different accounts altogether, in four different banks. Her name was on none of them, only Rolf's name. She found the account from which he gave her a strict cash allowance for groceries, and she had to account for every penny each week. The stubs showed the disbursements and the word "household." Her name was not even on the stub. She was "household" to Rolf.

Agatha used Rolf's calculator to add the four

account balances. The combined balances totaled $6,647,520.74. She felt herself gasping for breath and she saw spots for a moment. She put her head down and breathed slowly until she regained her composure.

This is cash, Agatha realized. *These accounts do not include any investments like stocks or real estate. I cannot understand why he would keep so much cash, but I know I have been an idiot. I have allowed him to make me poor when I am rich. I am very rich.*

She chose the bank whose branch was nearest to the house, only four blocks away. The balance there was close to a million and a half dollars, which would be sufficient. *Very sufficient*, Agatha thought.

She put on her lined raincoat, picked up her purse and walked downstairs and outside. The sun had finally cleared away the fog and she felt better, out and moving in the cool air.

She asked the woman at the New Accounts desk for a signature card for a checking account. She explained that she and her husband wanted to update the names on the account. The woman handed her a blank card. It was easy.

Back in Rolf's office, she looked at the check-book to see what branch held the actual account. She would have to take the new signature card there, where the current signature card was on file. Again, it was easy; the account's branch address was printed right there on the checks.

She pulled a letter from the correspondence file in the file cabinet and compared Rolf's signature at the bottom of the letter to the signature on the tiny checks photocopied in the bank statements. They matched, so Agatha knew Rolf did not sign checks any differently than he did correspondence.

She practiced on a pad of paper, and it did not take her long to create a quite credible signature for Rolf. She used his favorite fountain pen for the signature and then signed her name in a different ink. It helped that she had learned to write the same Germanic script that Rolf had practiced as a child. The "f" was distinctive.

The signature card ready, she walked to Geary Street and caught the 38 bus downtown. She walked along Kearney Street to California Street and then downhill to the bank. She handed over the signature card and the checkbook to the New Accounts person and all she had to do was show her driver's license with the address and last name the same as the one on the account, and that was that.

"Shall I order new checks with your name on them, Mrs. Hein? That will avoid any problem getting stores to accept checks from you. You should expect your ATM card in the mail within two weeks," said the nice man, handing her back the checkbook. "The PIN will be the same as your husband's."

He was so courteous and helpful. She assumed all bank employees were courteous and helpful to customers who kept a million-and-a-half dollars parked in a checking account.

Back at home, Agatha looked in Rolf's wallet on the dresser for the ATM card. There it was.

Agatha had never used an ATM but she knew that now all she needed was his PIN code. She went down to the desk and rummaged. No sign of the code in the checkbooks. She turned to the file cabinet and pulled up the file folder containing the bank statements.

There was nothing in the folder but the statements themselves. But what was that written on the folder tab? Oh, he could not be that stupid, could he? But of course he could: Four numbers; 2004 on all the account folders.

Once again it is so easy, Agatha thought. *It is the twentieth of April, his birthday, in the way we write it in Europe with the day of the month first.*

She put the ATM card in her pocket and walked four blocks back to the nearby branch. She had never used an ATM before, and she didn't know what to do. There were two people in front of her and she watched them. The woman in front of her caught her peeking over her shoulder and shifted her body to block Agatha's view. Agatha apologized and backed away.

When it was her turn, she fed the card into the slot upside-down, but the screen showed her a message and a picture of how to put the card in, and on the second try she got it right.

She held her breath as she pressed the keys for the PIN. Four digits, 2-0-0-4. Nothing happened. Could she have been wrong? She read the screen carefully. "Enter your PIN," it said. She looked down at the keypad and back up to the screen. She did not know what to do to make it keep going.

"Do you need more time?"

The screen showed the question and the machine beeped at her. She looked down at the keypad and saw the "Yes" key and pressed it. The screen asked her again to enter her PIN. This time, after she pressed the four keys, she spotted the green ENTER key on the keypad and pressed it.

After that, it was very straightforward. She decided to take one thousand dollars, so that she would not need to withdraw money for the next few days. She was not confident that managing the banking would continue to be so easy.

The machine disgorged a thick pile of twenties, and Agatha panicked. How could she carry all this money home? Anyone might see her walk away from the ATM and decide to rob her. She felt a wave of fear sweep through her as she folded the bills and shoved them into her coat pocket. She scanned anxiously for anyone who might have watched her, and hurried away with her hand still in her pocket, clutching the money.

I have to be more careful, she thought. *I have to do things that are more normal. I cannot make sudden changes like this. Everything must stay as it was. But of course,* she realized as the cool breeze from the Pacific swept her hair away from her face, *nothing will stay as it was.*

Such a relief. She took her hand out of her pocket and walked confidently with her long farm-girl stride toward her home.

≈11≈

I was reclining in the lounge chair gazing contentedly at my Japanese garden, sipping mint tea and keeping company with the two dogs and two cats. The dogs are burly, sturdy, one large and one small, one mostly black and one mostly brown. The cats are black, because apparently people are superstitious and tend to avoid adopting black cats from the shelter. I am not superstitious in that way, and when I rescue a cat it is always a black one.

The pets were curled up in various sunny spots on the deck. I could hear the constant rush and fade of the ocean. A breeze rustled the leaves of the tall trees beyond my fence. I could smell salt water and the evergreen smell of cypress trees.

I had changed into a heavy cotton sweater and a long loose skirt that reached the floor. On my feet were old leather sandals. It was cool out; the temperature in San Francisco exceeds seventy-five degrees maybe twenty times a year, and drops below fifty-five maybe thirty times. As was typical for January, it was cool and sunny at midday; the seasonal rains were holding off this year. I hiked up my skirt to get some sun on my legs.

Beyond the garden fence on the right was Sutro Park. The deck was just high enough off the ground for me to see over the rear fence to the Pacific and the horizon. Ten or fifteen miles out a big container ship was headed north. When big ships like that are visible so close to land, they are about to turn east into the Golden Gate and pass on to the Port of Oakland. I was watching to see when the ship turned east.

The afternoon was still pleasant; the wind that whips the fog into motion at tea time most days was not yet sweeping in, demanding that everyone put on a warm jacket or else.

I felt the urge to rake some sand. I was still fretting about Asa's reading. I usually forget cards as soon as the reading is over, but then I don't usually see cards like his. Raking the sand in my garden, making concentric parallel lines around the big smooth rocks, helps me calm down when I feel fretful.

I started down the steps to the garden. I heard

the garage door open, a surprise because I thought Thorne was with Asa. I turned to look as I stepped, and snagged the hem of my skirt with the heel of my sandal. My foot slipped on the slick leather insole of the loose shoe, and caught only the edge of the step. I heard a muted snap, like the pop you make with your fingers when you realize you've forgotten something, and I fell sideways into the sand. My foot had pronated off the edge of the step faster than my falling body could keep up with it, and my ankle had done what ankles do under those circumstances.

I sat up and looked at my foot, hanging off the end of my leg like fruit from a tree. I felt the bones grating against each other as I lifted my foot back into alignment with my leg.

"Two years," my inner voice said.

I'm pretty sure I had started yelling by then. Yelling curses, yes, I was undoubtedly cursing and yelling. I believe the dogs barked. I think Hawk was pressing his nose into my hair, snuffling my ear. I don't know where the cats went; I may have heard scrabbling claws on the redwood planks of the deck but I was not paying attention to the cats.

I watched my foot as I cradled it. I was unaware of anything else except that foot. My left ankle was puffing up and turning dark pink. I felt myself start to shake.

"Stay there. Do not move." Thorne rested his

hand on my head gently as he spoke.

I nodded without looking at him and stayed put as he disappeared very quickly back into the house. Staying put was definitely the best thing to do. I did not feel at all ambulatory. Ambulance, yes; ambulatory, no. I was still shaking, paying very close attention to my ankle and foot, holding them together with all my might.

He was gone for what seemed like forever, but, knowing Thorne, he was probably back in under fifteen seconds.

"I need to take off your sandal."

I am pretty sure I nodded, but I was also overhead looking down, floating a little bit above the two of us.

He could have been doing microscopic brain surgery, unbuckling the sandal strap, sliding it gently under the fingers holding my foot, setting the shoe down on the step behind him. He and I always worked together as if there were one brain operating four hands.

He had brought a shallow cardboard box, some bubble wrap, a utility knife, and duct tape. He very quickly cut long grooves into the cardboard and folded it into a narrow trough, open at one end and closed at the other. He taped the three long sides and end piece to hold them in place. He lined the box with bubble wrap.

"Ready?"

He was so calm it made me calm. I looked up

at him. I melted back down inside my body and looked out of my own eyes again. Holding my foot and leg together, I lowered them into the padded container he held in place for me. I could feel garden sand between the bubble wrap and my calf.

"Hold the box."

I held the box.

He tucked more bubble wrap around my ankle. When I saw him pick up the tape, I lifted the box a little higher and he wrapped duct tape around the arrangement in five different spots, tearing the duct tape with his teeth as he went along. When he was done taping he looked at the box and then at me. My leg and foot were snug and stabilized in their makeshift splint.

"Are you hurt anywhere else? Knee? Neck? Head? Arms?" He was touching me gently, examining the areas he was asking about.

"No. Just the ankle. I can tell it's gravel inside."

I leaned my head back, sniffed air into my nostrils, and swallowed tears. I had stopped crying but I was still shaking.

"Be right back." He went back into the house and returned with a blanket from his bed. He wrapped it around my shoulders.

"I'm all sandy."

"It doesn't matter. Put your right leg under the box to support it."

I slid my right leg under my left one. Thorne put one arm around my shoulders and the other under my knees and lifted me up. I am not an inconsequential specimen, at five feet nine inches and somewhere around one hundred thirty-five pounds. I might as well have been a laundry hamper half full of lacy lingerie for all the effort Thorne seemed to be expending carrying me up the steps to the deck and through the garage to the street.

"Hold on."

I put my arms around his neck. For a moment I forgot my ankle and appreciated why women fantasize about being carried effortlessly by big strong men. I smelled warm cotton and soap and man skin.

"Klaatu barada nikto," I said.

He laughed. His laugh is deep and explosive, and is a rare and delightful sound.

"You make Patricia Neal look like Shrek."

"Gort the beguiler."

We were both smiling now. I was no longer shaking.

At the curb Thorne lowered me enough that I could reach the back door of the Beemer and open it, and he slid me carefully onto the seat. He opened the front door and pushed the passenger seat control to slide the seat forward toward the dashboard, at the same time lowering the passenger seatback until it was almost reclining.

"Lift your leg onto that." I lifted my left leg onto the raised seatback so the cardboard trough was resting on the angled leather.

"Where is Asa?" I asked.

"With Don. Don't worry."

Don Madrone was another bodyguard. Thorne and I had met him while tracking a murderer, whom Don happened to be protecting at the time. He hadn't known he was guarding a murderer, so Thorne forgave him for working for a crook. Thorne had surprised and disarmed Don, after which they became pals and occasional co-workers.

Only buffoons seem to mind when Thorne outsmarts or overpowers them. Once disarmed or decked, people take it for granted that there was no way to reverse the outcome of the encounter and thus there are rarely hard feelings.

As if hard feelings would do any good.

"Why did you come home?" I asked.

"Don's got Asa. I needed to arrange for more guys. Don't worry."

Thorne folded himself into the front seat, pressed the control to close the garage door, and drove me to UCSF Medical Center, calling them *en route* to tell them we were on the way, what the injury was, and when to expect us.

He ended the call and looked at me in the rear view mirror.

"Morphine," he said, "is terrific."

He drove like the BMW was carrying a wounded President.

≈12≈

Agatha backed out of the garage, her eyes darting back and forth between the car's mirrors to check her clearance on each side. There were only inches to spare and she knew from experience that if the left mirror cleared the door jamb by more than six inches the right mirror would catch against the opposite side and snap backward. Slowly she cleared the doorway and backed out onto 48th Avenue.

She saw that big man, the renter at young Miss Bard's house, carry Miss Bard out of the house and lower her into the black BMW he drove. There was some sort of brown box taped to Miss Bard's leg.

There must have been a mishap there, she thought.

Agatha paused to watch, until the BMW pulled away quickly from the neighboring house and turned right onto Anza. Agatha thought she would stop by later to see if Miss Bard needed any help. Perhaps she should take over a casserole.

Now that Agatha had enough cash it was time for more errands from the list. She drove down the hill to the Great Highway along Ocean Beach and coasted through the timed signals at thirty-five miles per hour.

The ocean was gray and the waves were wild and uneven. *There must be a storm out at sea*, she thought. At Sloat Boulevard she turned left and then left again into the Garden Center parking lot.

A cubic-foot bag of fertilizer for the roses. Twenty plastic five-gallon containers for the shrubs to sit in while she reworked the soil. A pickax to loosen the dirt, and a sharp spade to dig the ground. A large plastic tarpaulin.

The roses would bloom only for her from now on, and she knew they would be especially gorgeous this season, once she had finished her work in the garden. She paid cash for everything and the nice associate with the green apron loaded her purchases into the trunk for her.

She drove next to Noriega Street, to one of the shops that sold housewares of all varieties and were operated by the many Asians living in the Richmond and Sunset Districts of San Francisco.

But now they live in all the districts, she thought.

She found a cleaver that had good balance in her hand and bought it to replace the one she had discarded. She decided to get a large blue storage bin with a snap-on lid. She picked up a box of one hundred pairs of latex gloves and a plastic apron as well. A real find on the jammed shelves was a box of light blue paper booties with white elastic around the top, like surgeons wear in a hospital.

As she was paying, the man at the register asked her if she was a "rearstay jen."

"Excuse me?"

"Rearstay jen. Brue shoe for open house inna rain."

"Oh yes, I see. Yes, yes," she said, nodding. "A real estate agent, yes. Thank you very much."

He put her purchases in the blue bin as he rang them up, snapped on the lid, handed her the receipt and thanked her. He bowed slightly as he handed her the change and receipt. She liked that.

She drove back along the Great Highway toward home. It was mid-afternoon now and the sun had dropped very low over the ocean. The sky was darker blue and fog had massed above the gunmetal gray water, flecked now with white foam where the waves broke.

Agatha realized she had not eaten since breakfast and she was ravenous. She did not want to cook. She wondered whether she would ever want to cook again.

There, just as the road turned east away from the ocean, sat the remodeled Cliff House. She had heard it was lovely inside, but much more expensive now. For a moment she hesitated, and then she laughed.

If lunch costs more than eight hundred dollars I will be in trouble, she thought. *Otherwise I will sit and enjoy myself.*

She made a U-turn into a parking space and climbed out of the car. She was glad everything in San Francisco was so casual, because she was not dressed up to go anywhere fancy. But the hostess could not have been more cordial, and led her to a table right at the window overlooking the ocean and Seal Rock, facing north to the Golden Gate.

It was slow at this time of day in the restaurant, and the waiter—one called them servers now, she realized, so they could be both men and women—brought her water with a lemon slice and asked if she would like a cocktail.

She decided against it. She had more work to do today.

He told her the specials. She chose the petrale sole and on a whim she asked for a glass of gewurztraminer. A glass of the slightly sweet wine would be so nice with the fish and would not affect her so much that she would be unable to finish her chores at home.

The busboy brought a basket of bread, warm and fragrant with rosemary, and cold sweet butter in a little ramekin. She took a bite, and thought nothing would ever taste as good as that soft, chewy bread with the melting butter.

She had not hurried this afternoon. Hurrying was what she normally did, rushing through the day to accomplish everything Rolf expected of her. She had dawdled at the garden center, mulling over the different types of fertilizer, reading labels, comparing prices on the plastic pots, pondering over the plants and flowers that might complement the roses come springtime.

Now, relaxing at her table as the sun sank toward the offshore fog, she watched as flocks of brown pelicans, wings outstretched as they glided across the waves in ragged skeins, swept northward toward the rocky islands where they would settle for the long cold night.

A towering container ship moved east into the Golden Gate. Its speed was deceptive; she thought it was moving slowly at first and then saw how rapidly it cleared the Marin County headlands and swept under the elegant dark orange bridge.

The waves were rough here. She could hear them pounding on the rocks below the restaurant. The rhythmic beating of the cold waves against the cliffs was calming, reassuring, but misleading, she knew.

Tourists were always climbing down and getting trapped or swept away by sudden high surf.

Sleeper waves, they were called, that looked like nothing and then loomed up suddenly and yanked your feet out from under you and dragged you out into the ruthless undertow and riptides from which there was no saving you. The currents here were cold and invincible, Agatha thought. Heartless.

Her fish arrived, with a lemon cut in half and netted so she could squeeze it without getting seeds on the grilled filet. There were tiny vegetables as well, little carrots and zucchini and summer squash, glistening with olive oil and still crisp in the center. She tasted butter and toasted pine nuts in the rice, a savory surprise. It had been a very long time since anyone had cooked for her. She ate everything slowly, tasting each bite and watching the sun turn vermilion as it sank below the horizon.

More people were coming into the restaurant now. When she had finished, the busboy—Agatha remembered they were called bussers now, even though they were always men—cleared her dishes and scraped up the breadcrumbs with a little curved blade.

The server arrived with a dessert menu and Agatha ordered apple tart and coffee. The noise of the other patrons swelled, and their conversations soothed her. The fog was billowing in from the sea, shrouding Bird Rock and Seal Rock until the craggy islands disappeared into the murk.

Through the plate glass she could hear the sea lions barking.

She remembered when she was a girl and her parents invited friends over during the quiet, dark winter months. She loved to curl up at the top of the stairs and listen to the visitors' voices as the party went on past her bedtime. She felt happy and secure hearing the chatter, and she loved the smells of cooked meat and bread and the cinnamon in the apple tart her mother made for a sweet. She would fall asleep listening to the reassuring buzz from downstairs.

Her parents, finding her on the landing when they came to bed, carried her, still sleeping, to her room and tucked her in.

This apple tart was almost as good as her mother's, Agatha decided. And the cinnamon ice cream was lovely. She ate all of it. Never waste food; she had grown up with this inviolable rule.

The server brought the bill and she paid cash, adding enough for a generous tip. She thanked the hostess as she walked past the podium, and in a daze of contentment she reached the sidewalk.

It was chilly now, the sky dark and the cold wind blowing damp fog across the Great Highway that stretched the six-mile length of the western beach of the City. The fog was heavy and wet, condensing on and dripping from the eaves of the restaurant and from the towering cypress trees across the highway in Sutro Park. The pavement glistened and moisture had beaded on the windshield and hood of her Mercedes.

Her Mercedes. Yes, the car was hers now.

She could smell the fertilizer from the trunk when she opened the car door. The car was cold inside; she switched on the seat warmer and turned the car's heater all the way up. She had only a few hundred yards to drive, up the hill and half a block to the right, but she was shivering as she pulled into her driveway. Just then the heater kicked in. She sat for a moment in the driveway with the engine running and let the heater blast out of the vents until she was warm again.

She unloaded the plastic bin and set it on Rolf's workbench. She tied on the plastic apron to protect her clothing and had no problem wrestling the heavy bag of fertilizer out of the trunk, dragging it across the cement floor to rest next to the green bags.

She untied the apron, hung it on a hook, and went upstairs to tackle the feather bed, to mend it so she could wash it and throw it away. On a whim she brought it down to the living room and sat on the carpet watching the pink floor paper burn in the fireplace.

Such a lively fire it was, and she quickly basted the fabric to close the bullet holes. She need not make as careful a job of it as she would have done under other circumstances, and soon she bit through the thread next to the final knot. She gathered up the escaped feathers and put them in the garbage can under the kitchen sink.

Agatha carried the unwieldy feather bed down to the garage to the deep sink and rinsed and scrubbed it with soap and cold water to remove the blood stains. It was a slow process, and water seeped far past the original stain into the rest of the feathers and fabric, but finally the stain had faded away.

She hung the feather bed to dry over a pipe near the furnace and went back upstairs to finish burning the pink floor paper. Her damp clothes dried as she knelt on the carpet facing the fireplace. Shadows around her in the living room leaped and fled in the dancing light.

For the first time in her married life Agatha realized that she felt safe. Overall, it had been a happy day. She felt a pleasure she had forgotten was possible. For once, she was unworried about what Rolf would say or do.

Tomorrow, Agatha thought as she stared at the cheerful fire, *Rolf will finally do something useful for those rosebushes he is so jealous of.*

She tore the last of the pink paper into pieces and fed it into the cheerful flames.

ב ב ב

Agatha awoke when the house wrens began to chirp at 5:30. She was confused at first. Why was she asleep in the guest room?

It came back to her then. Today was for mattress shopping, gardening, and tidying up the garage.

Rolf had always forbidden her to do more to the roses than cut stems for household flower arrangements. A cold, clear day loomed ahead of her, perfect for pruning, uprooting, and replanting the shrubs.

She was not afraid of the labor, of digging deep into the dirt around each shrub and straining to pull the recalcitrant plant out of the ground. As a young girl she had tended the kitchen garden at her family's farm. A lot of muscle power was called for, keeping the family fed with fresh fruits and vegetables all summer, and canning and drying the harvest at the end of each growing season. She had worked with her father in the fields, too, with the horses and later the tractor. She was strong and capable and sensible.

Today she would need a bigger vehicle than the car. She dressed in slacks and sweater again and ate a good breakfast of eggs and sausage and oatmeal.

She folded the now-dry tarp in the guest bathroom and carried it down to the garage, setting it next to the bedding bags. She moved the non-bedding bags out of the garage and into the garden, leaning them against the rear wall of the house and covering them with the new tarp to prevent any neighbors from wondering what they were. She weighed the tarp down with a brick at each corner.

She carried out the fertilizer, tools and the plastic pots and set them alongside the tarp. She placed the blue storage bin on a shelf in the garage. She wasn't sure what she would use it for. It was for just in case.

Back in the kitchen Agatha looked in the yellow pages and made a call to reserve a van. She would have to drive the Mercedes to the rental lot, leave it there, and come back for the car when the garden work was finished.

As she started the car, a thought struck her: how long would it take her to dig up all the roses? Certainly an entire day, perhaps more. That was too long. She wanted to have all the tasks on her list completed today, not just the rose garden.

She drove toward Gough Street, heading for Highway 101 south and the truck rental center. As she neared the on-ramp, she remembered the story in the newspaper about Hispanic day workers who gathered outside the Home Depot every morning, hoping someone would pick them up and pay them cash, usually not much per hour, for simple jobs.

She had cash. Cash was not a problem. She relaxed and pulled onto the highway.

≈13≈

I have incurred, according to the extremely hand-some third-year orthopedic resident in the UCSF emergency room, a bi-malleolar fracture with dislocation. What that means is the little ankle bumps on each side of my left foot have popped off the leg bones they belong to and, until the good doctor "reduced the dislocation," my foot was no longer connected to my leg the way the original blueprints indicate it is designed to be.

Before the first attempt to reconnect my foot to my leg, Thorne asked the resident, Dr. Lands, "What are you specializing in?" and Dr. Lands answered, "Orthopedics."

"Why?" asked Thorne.

Dr. Lands looked at Thorne and then at me.

"I like the idea of helping people walk again," he said.

Thorne nodded and sat down in the chair at the foot of the emergency room bed. It took a total of ten hours and three strong-arm wrangles by the orthopedist to get everything reconnected properly. The process: X-ray, strong-arm wrangling, quick-dry cast, pictures to see if everything is back where it is supposed to be.

No? Repeat.

No again? Repeat once more.

Yes? Go home now.

Oh, and here are prescriptions for opiates and laxatives, since you will want to continue taking opiates for the pain and those opiates are going to plug you up something ferocious.

Morphine does not actually reduce pain, based on this patient's experience. It does, however, an utterly dazzling job of making one not care in the least that the medical professionals crowded around one's foot attempting to manhandle it back into position over and over again are really hurting the holy fucking hell out of one.

The good news turned out to be that three rounds of wet-to-dry quick-setting casts had scraped all the sand off my leg, so I didn't feel like there were emery boards exfoliating me from knee to toe inside the final cast.

Thorne sat in the chair in the corner until the doctor and nurses took their first stab at wrangling my ankle back into place.

When I whimpered he stood quickly, and for

a moment I wondered dopily whether he would pull them off of me and damage them. Instead I saw him steel himself, clench his fists, lift his chair up over everyone's head and then slip around behind them to my side.

He sat down in the chair and took my right hand, the one minus the IV morphine drip. My normal-sized hand disappeared inside his gigantic one. He stayed by my loopy side, a massive, rough reassurance, for the long stuporous hours of the ordeal.

X-rays indicated surgery would be necessary in order to create a bionic ankle where until yesterday at midday there was a factory-installed one. Apparently this sort of injury, referred to by medical professionals as a "comminuted" or "smithereen" facture, requires bolts and screws in order to heal, with probably a slathering of surgical Krazy Glue and/or physician's Bondo dabbed here and there.

I asked if they could do the surgery with an endoscope through a dainty, almost-invisible incision in my belly button or kneecap or toenail, but no. I will be sporting some bodacious Frankenstein-esque scars by the time they have finished with me. My hopes of a career as a foot model are dashed. I may be doing the hokey-pokey at the TSA screening gate from now on.

It turns out the human ankle is simply not a very sturdy design, and is easily rendered into shards that simply will not reattach to each other if left to themselves to reconnect. My brother Brett was born with four teeth missing. That spontaneous mutation, since everyone tends to have their wisdom teeth yanked at some point, seems like it ought to be widely promoted. I now think ankles ought to be pushed to the top of the mutation wish list, along with the ability to metabolize dark chocolate at twice the rate of every other food.

By the time Dr. Lands was satisfied with the way things looked on the fluoroscope, it was three in the morning. He told me I was booked for an appointment with the fully fledged orthopedic surgeon the day after tomorrow.

My entire task for the foreseeable future, the ER ankle-wrangler said, would be to sit with my foot elevated higher than my heart, with ice on it to bring down the swelling. Until the eggplant-colored swelling went down there could be no surgery and resultant bionic-ness. Bionicity. Bionitude.

The hospital put me in a wheelchair to roll me to the waiting car Thorne had retrieved. It was not yet anywhere close to dawn and the neighborhood around the huge hospital was very still, the houses dark.

When we got home, Thorne carried me upstairs. I saw a little flash of Scarlett and Rhett and the wide red-carpeted stairway.

He moved to the front bay window my comfortable leather chair and an ottoman, atop which, for height, were two sofa cushions covered with a plastic garbage bag to keep them dry, plus a bath towel over the plastic to provide a non-skid absorbent surface.

Resting on that elevated, cushioned arrangement was my cast-encased ankle, perched on a gallon Zip-Lok bag full of ice. Another ice bag was draped across the upper surface of the cast, thereby forming a tidy little ice and ankle sandwich. My swollen ankle was cold and, I hoped, shrinking rapidly back to its normal circumference.

I could see Thorne inwardly debating the wisdom of duct tape judiciously applied to the ice bags. Large swaths of duct tape are so tempting for anyone with a Y chromosome, but I watched him realize that it would be more difficult for me to switch out the ice bags. He put the roll of tape down where it would remain handy.

Surrounding my chair were a small table, four books, a cooler holding bottled water as well as more bagged ice and a bagged egg salad sandwich. Arrayed within reach were a pile of dry towels, a plastic garbage bag for wet towels if the Zip-Loks leaked, a glass, a mug, a thermos full of mint tea, my laptop, my iPod and earbuds, my iPad, my purse, my cell phone and landline phone, a prescription bottle full of Oxycodone, a box of chewy oatmeal raisin cookies, a bag of assorted Ghirardelli dark chocolate squares, a plastic container of dried cranberries, a book of two hundred difficult crossword puzzles, a mechanical pencil with eraser, a quilted bag with multiple skeins of yarn and a size P rosewood crochet hook, the remote control, and the small flat-screen TV from Thorne's downstairs apartment. The TV was connected to a long black extension cable so I could view as many channels as I might wish.

Behind my head was a squashy pillow from my bed, and Thorne had tucked a crocheted afghan around me. On my right foot was a black shearling slipper with a ribbed non-skid sole. Before moving me to the chair Thorne and I had done what we could to shake the last of the sand off my clothes. As loopy as I was, I did not yet feel like essaying a wardrobe change.

I was thus thoroughly outfitted in my new command post because I was forbidden to put weight on my left leg. Lying alongside the chair were crutches on which to support myself getting back and forth to the bathroom. From my morphine-dazed experiment with them upon arriving home I gleaned that the entire purpose of the crutches was to cause me to break my other leg.

So I was effectively housebound. San Franciscans are not ranch-style people. I was sixteen steps up from the sidewalk, my car, the grocery store, my regularly patronized café, the park, dog-walking, and the ocean. The Pacific is my mental health practitioner of choice.

Even if I could navigate the steps by sliding up and down on my rear end, how was I supposed to navigate them with crutches? I was imagining ways to heave the crutches downstairs so they'd be waiting for me after I thumped down bum-wise step by step, okay fine. But how do I get me and the leg-breakers back upstairs when I arrive home? How do I purchase and carry groceries? Walk the dogs? Cook?

Well, okay, I never cook. But carry restaurant-delivered food to the command post from the kitchen? I had no desire to do any of those things immediately, but at some point the morphine would wear off and I would be marooned in the chair for weeks and weeks.

I was going to have to find a way back out into the world. I need the world.

I had asked Thorne to set me up next to the front window of the living room so that should I wish to I could watch the people and traffic going by on 48th Avenue.

For the time being I did not feel any avid desire to look out the back window at the Japanese garden, scene of the ankle atrocity.

Hawk and Kinsey, the dogs, were sitting alongside the chair for the time being, because they were quite certain I was going to need to pet them very soon and that petting them would assist me in mending my ankle more rapidly. Dogs appear to be certain that our petting them helps us do everything we need to do in life, plus I think they are confident it will lead to universal nuclear disarmament or a biscuit, either one a worthwhile outcome, with biscuits having a distinct edge.

Meeka and Katana were asleep in their kitty bed, curled around each other. While I was fading in and out, Thorne had fed them all and had walked the dogs. He was gone now. I assumed he had called in the troops he needed and headed out to organize the protection of Asa and his sister.

I was awake at one point, gazing desultorily out the big window. Across the street and a few houses up, I saw Mrs. Hein back a U-Haul panel van into her driveway. Two dark-haired men wearing jeans and windbreakers climbed out and went into her garage with her.

Mrs. Hein unlocked the van's rear doors. The men began to carry dark plastic garbage bags to the van and throw them in. I counted four full bags before I saw Thorne's car pull up to the curb below the window.

The garage door downstairs rumbled.

I watched Thorne uncoil himself from the front seat and open the car's rear door and trunk. He had showered and changed clothes at some point; he was wearing gray jeans, buff work boots and a darker gray oxford cloth dress shirt.

He pulled a folded walker and a paper bag from the rear seat. From the trunk he lifted out two wheelchairs. Out of the open sunroof he pulled two long wooden rounds, like three-inch-thick twelve-foot dowels, and tucked them under his arm. They bent into an arc, like the balance pole Philippe Petit carried on his high-wire walk between the Twin Towers.

Wheelchairs slung over one arm and dowels and walker under the other, he disappeared into the garage. He came upstairs with one wheelchair and the walker.

"The walker is in your bathroom. One of the wooden stools from the kitchen is in the shower," he said. "The wheelchair is for everywhere else upstairs. Once you're not morphined to the gills I'll bring you a knee walker, to use indoors only. Give me a minute to get things set up."

"How is Asa?"

"Fine."

"The doctor said I can't put weight on this for at least six weeks, probably longer."

"We'll figure it out." He put his hand on my shoulder.

"Okay," I said, looking up at him.

He doesn't usually touch me, as I said. I don't know whether it was the Oxycodone or just the weight of it, but I could still feel the pressure of his hand after he walked away. I liked the feeling.

I was using some fabulous drugs though. I

liked just about everything right then.

Thorne disappeared down the stairs. For the next half hour I heard sawing and drilling and hammering from the stairway.

With my eyes half-closed I watched the men at Mrs. Hein's finish loading the garbage bags. They disappeared again into the garage. Opiates and the long sleepless night with the ankle wranglers had me nodding off as the noise from my stairway continued.

I felt Thorne's hand on my shoulder and opened my eyes.

"Dry run. I'll spot you," he said.

"What do I do?"

He handed me a pair of leather gloves. I looked at them dopily.

"No blisters," he said.

He hovered as I donned the gloves and hoisted myself out of the easy chair. He made sure I locked and unlocked the wheels before standing up from or sitting down into the wheelchair. The cast slipped off the wheelchair's foot rest, so he lifted off both footrests and set them aside.

My ankle throbbed when I lowered it. I made a noise and lifted my leg back into the air. He held up his hand for me to wait and went downstairs. He returned with a one-by-six plank, spare lumber remaining after we built out his apartment's kitchen/living area. He slid the plank under me in the wheelchair, placing a throw pillow on top as a cushion. I sat on the cushion and extended my left foot out onto the plank.

Better.

I wheeled the chair to the stairs. Thorne carried the crutches to the bottom and turned back to face me. He had installed the dowels as a second handrail across from the existing metal rail. There was a gardener's kneeling pad, shaped like a shoe box lid, resting on the top step.

"Lock the wheels. Stand up and grab the handrails. Turn around so you're facing away from the stairs and kneel on the pad with your left knee," he said. I did what he'd told me to do.

"Feel behind you with your right foot for the lowest step you can reach safely. Hold on with both hands so you feel secure, and push yourself upright so you're standing on your right foot."

I used my arms to push myself up onto one leg, my left knee flexed flamingo-fashion. I was facing up the stairs, standing on my right leg three steps from the top, gripping the handrails to keep myself steady.

"Hold on with one hand and bring down the knee pad. Maybe one step up from your right foot?"

I did that. I kept it up, stepping down backwards, pushing myself up onto my right foot, bringing down the pad and kneeling on my left knee, until my right foot was on the ground. By using both handrails I could control how slowly or rapidly I stood up or knelt.

Handing the crutches to me, he said, "Get to your car. Pop the trunk."

It was only ten feet to the door of my beloved Chrysler 300C. I love that car with a mighty love.

"The Hemi engine is a safety feature," Thorne once told me, and I had solemnly agreed.

I leaned on the car and opened the driver's door, reaching in to push the trunk release button. Thorne stood nearby monitoring.

I knew where this exercise was headed now. Using the crutches to hop to the trunk, I opened it and sat on the lip of the trunk next to one tail light. Thorne had loaded the second wheelchair into the trunk. I rested the crutches against the fender and twisted my body around, using both arms to heave the folded wheelchair out onto the garage floor.

"How do I open it up?" I asked.

"Pull the arms apart. Lock the brakes."

I did that. When I stood up and the rear end of the car lifted, the crutches fell to the concrete floor.

Once I was in the chair, I picked up and loaded the crutches into the trunk. Simple.

"Now in reverse," he said.

Lift the crutches out, lean them on the fender, stand, turn, sit on the edge of the trunk, listen to the crutches fall down, lift up the center of the canvas wheelchair seat to fold the wheelchair, twist around and heave the chair back into the trunk, grab the fallen crutches, stand up, shut the trunk, hop on the crutches to the stairs, left knee/right foot/haul with my arms, left knee/right foot/haul with my arms, and turn and sit down into the wheelchair waiting on the top step.

"The docs signed a handicapped parking permit request. Wheelchairs can use the DMV appointment line," Thorne said. "I'm putting the form in the car, along with a backpack you can hang off the handlebars of the wheelchair."

"Got it. I'm going to wait until I'm cleaned up and okay to operate heavy machinery before I head to the DMV."

He looked at me. I was a little teary-eyed, realizing Thorne had given me my freedom when I had thought I was imprisoned for the next couple of months or more.

I made the effort to bring my emotions under control. He waited, his arms at his sides, looking up the stairs at me.

"Go," I told him. "Thank you. I'm all set now. Do your job."

Thorne believes whatever I tell him. It behooves me, therefore, to tell him the truth. Sometimes telling the truth proves uncomfortable for both of us.

This time, for instance, I did not say that I wanted him to stay, even though I very much wanted him to stay. There really was nothing else for him to do here; nonetheless I wanted him to stay. I wanted to hold his rough hand while I slept off the morphine.

Thorne, a discerning fellow, knows if I'm leaving anything out when I tell him the truth. Or maybe the morphine caused my brain to emit magic thought rays readable by anyone within a fifteen-mile radius.

I realized something had shifted between us during the last twenty-four hours.

He came up the stairs two at a time, touched my shoulder once more, then went back down and out the front door.

I rolled myself to the command post chair and hoisted myself into it. Across the street the panel van was still parked in Mrs. Hein's driveway.

Time passed. I dozed.

I awoke to the sound of the van's doors slamming shut. Agatha Hein and the two men had climbed into the cab. I saw her pulling on her seat belt. Her garage door slid shut and she drove away toward Geary Boulevard.

≈14≈

Agatha was satisfied with the work the men had done. The van had been loaded with the cut-up mattress, washed linens, headboard fabric and batting, curtains, and feather bed. The roses were pruned, dug out, and resting in plastic pots. Fertilizer had been sprinkled into the waiting holes in the ground.

She had dropped the workmen off after paying them so much money that they tried to give some back. She had then driven the garbage bags to the dump near Candlestick Point, and returned the rented van.

There had been no problem using the credit card from Rolf's wallet to rent the van; she had only to show her driver's license. When she returned the van, she paid cash and watched them cancel the credit card charge. She did not want a record of Rolf's card being used in San Francisco when she had told his office he had left town. Even so, why shouldn't a wife use her husband's card? She would have to think about this more later.

Now it was just one o'clock. She needed to drive to the mattress store right away. They advertised same-day delivery if you bought a mattress by two o'clock.

She was hungry, but she could ignore her appetite for another hour. Or she could get fast food at the drive-thru and eat it in the car on the way to the store. Rolf would have had a flaming Teutonic conniption at that idea. Yes. Fast food on the way to the mattress store sounded like a wonderful idea.

There would be time before the mattress was delivered to buy batting and fabric for a new headboard and curtains. She would need a new feather bed, comforter and duvet cover as well. She would work on sewing in the afternoon until the mattress arrived. After it was set up, she would make the bed with clean, smooth sheets. Tonight, after finishing the gardening and taking a lovely hot bubble bath, she would reclaim the master bedroom for herself.

All in all she had made a good plan and everything was proceeding smoothly. She put the car in gear and drove to the mattress store.

After selecting and buying a marvelously comfortable pillow-top mattress and getting an estimated delivery time, Agatha drove downtown to Union Square and parked in the underground garage. It was so nice to drive everywhere, to not have to wait outside in the changeable weather for busses.

She walked into Britex Fabrics and spent time selecting the polished cotton with which she would replace the bedroom curtains, headboard cover and duvet. She bought the batting and notions she would need and carried her purchases in the strong black and white Britex shopping bags back to her car.

Home to the roses, she thought, slipping the paid ticket into the parking garage machine and watching the barrier rise up into the air. She turned right onto Geary and cruised slowly past the theaters. Perhaps she would see a play one night this week. Or perhaps the opera or ballet. All the amusements that had been denied her for so long were suddenly hers to divert herself with. She would have to plan for them now that her evenings were free and she had money to spend on the best seat in the house.

At home she changed into her gardening clothes, and then stopped. She could not do the gardening now. It would have to wait until dark.

The houses on every San Francisco block crowd the front sidewalk in order to leave room for back yards. Back yards adjoin throughout the midsection of every block, separated by fences like cased wine bottles divided by cardboard. From any house's second story one could view the neighbors' gardens for half a dozen lots in either direction.

She would start with the sewing now and take care of the roses once the afternoon grew dark. Thank God it was wintertime and she would not have long to wait for the sun to set.

Replanting the roses would be a chilly job, but she was a fast worker and the work would keep her warm.

≈15≈

I had been dozing all morning, on and off. A little after midday I rolled to the kitchen to let the dogs out into the side yard for a few minutes. I wasn't very hungry—another big positive for the opiates—but I ate the egg salad sandwich from the cooler once I had settled back into the command post chair.

I was focused on my primary mission: elevate and ice the left ankle.

Mrs. Hein came home from her panel van adventure. She pulled the Mercedes into her garage and the door slid down. I was surprised to see her driving the car; usually her husband drove the Mercedes and whenever I saw her she was walking back and forth to the shops up on Geary.

Not much else was happening on the street.

Dog walkers had picked up their clients' pets
from three of the neighboring houses and driven
them off for a couple of hours of running around
Fort Funston with a pack of other doggy clients.

I wondered idly who I could pay fifteen dollars a day to for arranging a couple of hours of
hilarious social interaction with frolicsome, ener-
getic pals.

Whenever I left home for an out-of-town trip
the Pooch Patrol would take care of my pets. The
dogs knew the sound of the truck when it came to
pick them up for their sleep-over rollick with their
canine cronies, and they ran downstairs to the
door and wagged their tails so fast I thought they
would propel themselves through the wooden
barrier that was standing between them and their
chums.

The cats always stayed home; the Pooch Patrol crew fed them *in situ* while I was gone. The
cats did not get to rollick with pals, but then cats
are so rarely guilty of a good rollick. Plus they
tend not to enjoy the company of new pals, hiss-
ing and raising their hackles rather than collegial-
ly sniffing all available butts.

I no longer felt the urge to doze. I rolled myself to the bathroom, stripped, and, seated on the
kitchen stool with my leg perched on the walker,
tied a white kitchen garbage bag around the top
of the cast. Without mishap I managed to close
the curtain, stick my left leg out past the curtain,

and rest the cast on the top edge of the walker. I used the hand-held attachment to shower and rinse off the last of the sand; I washed and dried my shoulder-length blonde hair.

I pulled on a clean pair of stretchy black yoga pants; they were the only pants that would slide over the cast. In the narrow closet I could just reach the high clothes rod for a blue tank top and a black zip-front hoody. On my right foot I wore a cotton sock and a blue and white running shoe, not that I would be running anytime soon.

I rolled the wheelchair down the hall and sat back down in the command post chair. I elevated and iced my left ankle. I felt myself to be an independent woman, mistress of myself and my surroundings. Okay then. I took stock of my accomplishments so far that day.

I had washed and dressed myself.

I had observed Mrs. Hein and the workmen.

I had crocheted while watching television.

I had read some of a very good Ross Thomas novel, but then all his books are good.

I had eaten.

I had swallowed a half-tab of Oxycodone when the ankle became obstreperous.

I had dozed.

I had sipped mint tea.

I had added ice to the ice bags.

I had worked a crossword puzzle involving atrocious puns.

I had e-mailed my friends and family to inform them of my status and, except from my Mother, had received prompt replies full of sympathy and kind offers of visits and assistance. I replied to them all saying I would call with more news after the doctor's appointment.

Yolanda did not ask what I needed; my tax accountant and true friend, she wrote an email from her Oakland high-rise office saying she would be over after work with macaroni and cheese. Yo-Yo never wastes time offering; she just does what she perceives with her very astute perception to be necessary. I love Yo-Yo and her astuteness. Also her mac and cheese.

I had not had to call my boss; I have no boss right now. It's a long story, involving a large legal settlement in my favor. Right now I am not gainfully employed, nor do I need to be gainfully employed in order to remain financially solvent.

For now, the third-grade class I sponsor would have to proceed in my absence with the curriculum administered by the capable Mr. Schafer, a fine teacher, who e-mailed me that the kids would spend time learning about the human skeleton in my honor.

I was seated in a comfortable chair and every possible need had been anticipated and met for me, not to mention I was loaded on primo opiates. I was not scheduled to see the surgeon until tomorrow.

Really, I could not have been clearer that for the foreseeable future I was to sit with my left ankle elevated and iced, an unambiguous job description if ever there was one. Going out into the world at this point was a violation of the primary mission.

I was, nonetheless, suffering severely from that cognitive versus behavioral dissonance thingy. Cognitively, I could not have been clearer that elevating and icing were the primary mission. Behaviorally, after twelve hours or so of the primary mission, all I wanted was to be doing absolutely anything on earth other than elevating and icing.

Opiates, it turns out, do nothing to alleviate bat-shit boredom. As with pain, they make one not care so much that one is bored, but one is nonetheless foggily aware of one's actual monotonous condition.

My cell phone rang. I didn't recognize the number. I answered anyway. A telemarketer would represent a ripple of change in the bat-shit boredom.

It was not a telemarketer; it was Asa. "Can you get yourself down to Menlo Park? I would like your take on some things here. Thorne said you were injured, but he thought it would be okay if I asked."

"Can I please come there right now? Pretty please?"

He laughed. "He says to tell you there's ice."

"I'm on my way." I hoisted myself into the wheelchair, grabbed my purse and jacket and rolled to the stairs.

I was actually going to jump—well, crawl and hop—into the car and drive off without asking where I was going. Under the influence of opiates, I was content to aim for the Peninsula and use antenna-power for the fine-tuning, navigationally.

"Thorne says he called DeLeon," Asa said. "He says you're not supposed to operate heavy machinery."

"Oh. What a splendid idea."

The doorbell rang. I looked down the stairwell and through the window over the front door I saw DeLeon's black cap and Lincoln Town Car.

"Awesome," I said, and clicked off the phone. I neglected to say goodbye. I neglected to say thank you. I slung my purse over my shoulder, stood up, and grabbed the handrails so I could back down the stairs. My left ankle throbbed.

In my head I heard Aretha singing, "Freedom. Freedom. Freedom. Oh oh Freedom!"

I willfully declined to notice that the title of that song is "Think."

בבב

DeLeon Davies is the world's coolest human, bar

none; you can have your Johnny Depps and Lenny Kravitzes. Six feet tall, solidly built, with skin the color of baked pecans and graying hair combed back from his face, he sported diamond stud earrings and a jazzy necktie with his black suit, black shoes, black socks, black chauffeur's cap and crisp white shirt.

I have never heard DeLeon raise his voice louder than is absolutely necessary to be heard by a passenger in the back seat of his limousine. DeLeon has honed—nay, perfected—the art of anticipating whatever you are going to want and having it ready before you know you want it.

"Baby girl, what have you been up to now?" he said when I, leaning on crutches, opened the door.

Over the many years we have traveled together we have dispensed with "Ms. Bard" and "Mr. Davies." He was holding his arms out as if to catch me, although I was not at this point falling. No guarantees though, and, being DeLeon, he was anticipating.

"It's just a mess, DeLeon. Never mind about it."

"I know better than to guess how you want to handle this," he said. "You have your own ways. So you just tell me what you want and we'll take it from there."

I hopped on the crutches to the Town Car. He walked next to me with his arms held out as I wobbled across the sidewalk between my front door and the limousine.

"I'm loaded on Oxy," I said. "I can get myself into the car but I have no idea where I'm going. Did Thorne tell you where to take me? I might fall asleep on the way. Oh! It's nice to see you."

I turned, lifted up my arms to hug him, and the crutches rattled to the sidewalk. DeLeon grabbed my shoulder and steadied me.

"He told me where we're drivin'," DeLeon said. "Let's get you into the car now."

He gripped my hands to support me as I lowered myself into the back seat. He picked up the crutches and put them in the trunk once I was safely down.

"I'm to go up and fetch a cushion and ice from your livin' room," DeLeon said. "But first let's get you settled. Can you scoot on over?"

I slid across the back seat. He adjusted the front passenger seatback as Thorne had done the day before in the BMW.

"I'll be just a minute," he said, and headed into the house. Soon my left leg was an elevated and iced sandwich again, resting on the sofa cushion DeLeon had placed on the reclined front seat. He tucked my black leather jacket across my lap "for your privacy," he said, even though I was wearing pants. He pointed out the bottled water in the drink holder and asked me if I needed anything else.

"Nothing," I told him, for I was no longer marooned; I was outside in the wonderful world again, with trees and sky and fog and flowering shrubbery and a cool breeze carrying the aroma of ocean with it.

He drove smoothly—everything DeLeon does is smooth—east on Anza and then south toward Sunset Boulevard and the cruise down Highway 280 to the Peninsula.

"I want to know what happened to you if you want to tell about it," DeLeon said.

"I fell. My ankle broke into little bitty bits. End of story so far."

"Okay then. I thought you mighta been leapin' from the Acapulco cliffs into the arms of some Brazilian bodybuilder boyfriend."

"From now on that's what I'll tell people," I laughed. "Much better than saying I missed my footing on the step down to the yard."

"What brings you out on this junket? Shouldn't you be takin' it easy?"

"It's a long story, but the upshot is there's a client who's hired Thorne and now me to work with him, and there are some immediate problems he wants me to help him with."

"All right, all right. Thorne said he'll bring you home later today, but you know to call me anytime you need a driver. It's not busy this week at the hotels."

"Thank you, Mister Dee." I paused to think

how to ask him what I hoped he would find a way to answer. In addition to his skills and personal magnetism, DeLeon is a man of excessive and wide-ranging knowledge. Once long ago, apologizing for prying, I asked him why he still drove when I knew he had amassed more than enough to retire on, and he said, "I would miss all my peeps. They keep me up to date on what-all's happenin'."

"I know you don't talk about your clients, DeLeon, but I have a question, so just tell me if I'm out of line here, okay?"

"What is it Miz X?"

"This client of mine is starting up a company working with nanoparticles, nanorobots, stuff like that."

"Lotta that goin' on."

From past conversations I knew that DeLeon was a savant about virtually everything there was to know about every start-up since Hewlett-Packard.

"What do you hear lately?"

He mulled for a few seconds. "Any particular industry? That shit is everywhere, changin' every nanosecond."

He glanced in the rear view mirror, acknowledging that he was broadening his argot although still operating in his professional capacity.

"Medical applications. Tissue regeneration. Organ transplants," I said. "That shit."

He thought for a moment. "There's talk. Some trade papers, some clients."

He paused again, to think about what more he could say.

"Word is there's somethin' major goin' on. There's a race for a way to get organ transplants happenin' faster. All these boomers gettin' old, wantin' new livers and kidneys and hearts, not wantin' to wait their turn in line. Not wantin' the wait to be so long they never get their turn. Stories on TV about poor people overseas sellin' a kidney, black market for organs, that kind of mess. Steve Jobs dyin' of pancreatic cancer and gettin' a liver transplant along the way brought the question front and center about who gets to go first. That kid in China supposed to've sold his kidney for an iPad—there's all kind of craziness."

"Thorne and I are working for BioMorphic Technologies."

"That's where he told me to take you. Word is, they're in this deep. Maybe leadin' the pack."

"What's the main event? If you can call out a main event from all the craziness."

"There's a lot of attention on supply and demand. People donate their blood and companies sell it for hundreds of dollars a pint. People donate their organs and hospitals charge through the roof for a transplant. Hospitals goin' for-profit instead of non-profit changed everything. All that money to be had and no product to sell."

DeLeon shook his head at the sorryness of the mess.

"So the money to be made, that's the main event?" I asked.

"Be scads of money, always the main event."

"And where there be scads of money…"

"There be scads of scoundrels."

≈*16*≈

By four o'clock two men had delivered and in-
stalled the new mattress. They had been a little
surprised that there was no old mattress to haul
away, but she had tipped them each twenty dollars and they left cheerfully enough, saying thank
you as they walked down the front steps.

Agatha drove to the big linens store and
bought a new feather bed, sheets, and down comforter. Back at home, she washed and dried the
sheets, ran them through the mangle, and then
remade the bed.

Waiting for the mattress delivery, she had
made a good start on the new curtains and had
carried the stripped headboard into the sewing
room, ready for new batting and upholstery. The

unstained old fabric and batting had gone away with the other trash, just in case. There was nothing to worry about there.

Darkness had finally fallen; in January dusk came at five o'clock. She decided it was safe now to replant the roses. Agatha changed into one of Rolf's tan denim coveralls, the ones he wore when washing the car. She would have no compunction about washing and tossing out the coveralls when this next task was crossed off her list.

She laced up an old pair of running shoes that she would not miss when she threw them away, and she slipped blue paper booties over them. She pulled on a new pair of latex gloves and tucked her hair up in a shower cap.

Down in the yard she stood next to the rear wall of her house and looked up at the windows of the houses in back of and alongside hers. Most of the windows were in bedrooms, she knew, since most of the houses were roughly, or sometimes exactly, the same design. People would not turn in until nine or ten o'clock, which gave her at least four hours to empty the garbage bags and replant the roses.

She could not turn on the outdoor garden light. She dared not add to the risk of being seen. She would have to work with the illumination from her neighbors' windows and from the gibbous moon just rising over the rooftops ahead of her.

She lifted and gingerly set aside the bricks holding down the corners of the tarp, then pulled and folded the tarp very slowly to avoid the swishing sound it would make if she was not careful.

She slowly picked up the first of the twenty garbage bags, one for each rose bush hole. This would have to be a slow, steady, careful job, not the usual race she was accustomed to running for Rolf.

She decided to begin at the farthest part of the garden, working her way toward the house so that as she grew tired she would have fewer foot-steps to travel carrying the garbage bags. Lift the bag, carry the bag, untie the bag, fold back the bag, fill the hole with the garbage that was in the bag, pick up the rose bush, tuck down the rose's roots, tamp soil around the rose, fetch another bag.

She would water the roses tomorrow. They needed water after replanting but watering was too noisy, and watering at night risked mildew dusting and devouring the leaves.

Agatha had had the workmen yesterday sprinkle into the holes some of the fertilizer she had bought at the garden store. The men had placed the uprooted shrubs in the plastic five-gallon pots on the dirt next to the holes, so the concrete pathway was clear to walk. She had had to tell the men more than once that she did not want them to replant the roses for her. They had looked at each other in bewilderment; why would the lady want them to do only half of the work?

She took careful, quiet footsteps carrying the bags, hefting them away from her body so the plastic would not rustle against the coverall fabric.

She did not use the spade or trowel for fear they would scrape on the concrete path or the brick border. She needed a strong grip to keep the bags from slipping out of the latex gloves.

She did not want that nosy Mrs. Partierre calling the police again, telling them that first there are gunshots and now she's burying things in the garden at night. Agatha realized Mrs. Partierre would have noticed the roses in their plastic pots, and would wonder how they were replanted without her having seen it happen.

Agatha decided that if Mrs. Partierre asked about it she would laugh and tell her it was the rose fairies who had come and done it, like the tooth fairy, and would change the subject to Mrs. Partierre's son. Mrs. Partierre couldn't resist bragging about her son the eye doctor.

Agatha dropped an open bag. In the process of shifting it from the wall of the house to the next open hole she had allowed her attention to wander and the bag had slipped out of her gloved hands. Something had spilled onto the concrete; she could not see clearly what it was.

She picked up everything she could see and shoved it into the waiting hole. She would have to use the hose after all. She marked the spot by setting an empty plastic pot on the concrete just above the dark splotch.

Three hours later she had replanted all twenty roses. She breathed a sigh of relief at being finished in plenty of time, before the neighbors went to bed.

She rinsed her gloved hands in the deep sink next to the washer, collected the empty green garbage bags, folded them so their open ends were tucked inside, and stuffed them all into a new, clean bag. She tied the new bag shut and put it in the garage, ready to be walked to the dumpster behind the Geary Boulevard grocery store later tonight.

She had never handled any of the bags without wearing gloves. The workmen may have touched one of them by mistake, but good luck to the police, she thought, trying to track down one of the illegal immigrants by matching up fingerprints.

In the garage Agatha took off her shower cap and rinsed it in the deep sink. Still wearing the gloves, she went back outside and folded the tarp into a tight square, bringing it into the garage and putting it on the shelf where Rolf had kept the previous one. She could use this tarp to cover the Mercedes, or for other things.

In the garden she stacked all but one of the now empty five-gallon pots against the outside wall of the house. She would rinse those in the morning, checking for any marks left from her gloves during the replanting.

She rinsed and stripped off the gloves, dropping them in the sink, and went back outside. With her bare hands she turned on the hose and sprayed the pathway where the bag had spilled. She rinsed the walk for five minutes before deciding any evidence must have washed down the drain at the corner of the house. She carried the "marker" pot to the stack of others and placed it on top.

In the garage she rewashed her hands, took off the coveralls and shoes, and started them in the washer with detergent, bleach, and cold water. She threw the rinsed latex gloves into the garbage bin; no one would look twice at an old pair of gloves.

That was it, then. All the garbage disposed of. It had smelled, as garbage always does, but it was out of the house now and being put to good use with the roses.

Agatha went upstairs to put on slacks and a sweater. She pulled on a heavy jacket for the walk to the grocery store dumpster. Back in the garage, she slid on a new pair of latex gloves, reached into a cupboard for the hand-held garage door control and slid it into her jacket pocket. She picked up the green bag holding the other bags, and opened the garage door.

It was a short walk. No one saw her drop the bags into the grocery store dumpster.

She went back to the house and upstairs to look in Linda's purse for car keys. Finding them, she took her own purse and put on her jacket and headed outside to find Linda's car. Standing on her front step, Agatha pressed the unlock button on the key fob and, sure enough, a small sedan across the street blinked its lights. A car as cheap as the owner, Agatha thought. She climbed in and drove the car to the airport's long-term parking lot, left the keys in the ignition and the parking ticket on the seat, and caught a taxi home. Linda's clothes and purse, minus her wallet, Agatha packed up to drop off at the Salvation Army on Valencia Street the next day.

Agatha felt profound exhaustion settling into her body. It had been a long day full of hard work and she was sore in her shoulders and back from the exertion, but the work was finally finished. After a nice relaxing bubble bath she planned to order Thai food from a nearby restaurant and cross more tasks off her list.

She decided to learn how to eat with chopsticks. She must start a list of things she wanted to learn to do, now that she had figured out how to dispose of dead people.

Chopsticks would be a snap compared to that.

⪡17⪢

DeLeon pulled off Highway 101 at Marsh Road and swung around east over the freeway toward San Francisco Bay. He pressed buttons on his cell phone and said, "We're pullin' up." He looked at me in the rear view mirror.

"I have to say, Miss Bard, I'm surprised you got yourself hurt the way Mister Ardall looks after you."

We turned into the parking lot of a nondescript white one-story stucco and glass building in one of the business parks strewn throughout this area east of the highway, in the flat landfill next to San Francisco Bay.

"He wasn't home when it happened, but when it happened he was there instantly," I said. "I don't know how he does that."

"You two together yet?"

He raised his eyebrows and looked at me in

the rear-view mirror. Ahead of us, at the entrance to the building, Thorne stood holding a black five-wheeled conference room chair.

"DeLeon, we have discussed this topic before. You know very well that I have resigned permanently from the romance field of endeavor."

"Not any of my bidness. But it is mighty funny to see you go all Miss Daisy on me. And meanwhile, look at that man, standin' there waitin' on you."

"Not too heavy on the brake, please, Hoke," I said as he pulled to a stop and unlocked the doors.

Thorne rolled the chair up to the car and opened my door. DeLeon swapped the crutches he had pulled out of the trunk for the folded bill Thorne brought out of his pocket and passed to DeLeon somewhere in the midst of a convoluted handshake.

The two men did not bump chests or anything, but then if you try to bump chests with Thorne you either bump against his belt buckle or have to leap like a dolphin at Sea World aiming for a fish.

I grabbed the handle over the door and pulled myself out of the car onto my right foot, then turned and sat down into the waiting chair. The men flanked me and held their arms out alongside me in case that would assist me in becoming safely repositioned.

I stood up again to kiss DeLeon on the cheek and hug him goodbye.

"Thank you, sweetie. What you were telling me about the scoundrels is going to be important, I think."

"You call me now," he said to both of us, opening the front passenger door to reposition the front seat out of the way of subsequent fares with undamaged ankles. He handed me the sofa cushion and ice bags. He draped my leather jacket around me and patted my shoulders.

He did not bother to urge Thorne to take good care of me; DeLeon knew more than most people what Thorne would do. The gleaming Lincoln glided smoothly out to the street and was gone.

Asa was in the lobby. He clucked over my ankle and took in the heap of accoutrements I'd hauled with me on my trek to Silicon Valley.

"No room in the car for the kitchen sink?" he asked.

From the lobby Thorne rolled me through double doors and down a beige-carpeted aisle into a medium-sized conference room where Don Madrone was sitting with the woman I had visualized when I was reading Asa's cards. Asa introduced us and I held onto the table as I stood up to shake her hand, because she had stood up to shake mine.

Beth was an eerie ringer for her brother, and yet she was clearly female. She had the same smooth, slender fingers, olive skin, dark straight hair the same length and style as her brother's, black eyes that shone with identical intelligence, and she was the same height. They were even wearing similar clothes in similar colors.

Thorne wheeled me to the far side of the table from the conference room door and put my crutches down on the floor along the wall behind me. No chance of crutch clatter.

There was room for eight or ten people at the wood table, which was the color of a varnished baseball bat. I turned the chair next to me around and loaded the seat up with sofa cushion and ice, on top of which I lifted the bulky leg-filled cast, presenting it to everyone else at the table. I wiggled my pink polished toenails in a cheerful greeting. Wiggling hurt, so I ceased wiggling.

Thorne took up a position next to the door, standing and watching the area outside the room. Don moved to the end of the table behind Beth. Asa sat at the end near Thorne, facing me and his sister.

"Would you like some water? Or some coffee or tea?" Beth asked me.

"No thank you." I refrained from requesting a morphine drip.

Asa placed a stapled sheaf of papers in front of me. The quartet watched in silence as I read the non-disclosure agreement and signed the last page. I handed it back to Asa.

Everyone sat and waited. I was the pattern of all patience, which turns out to be a pretty easy pattern to be when there are whup-ass opiates in use.

"Asa," said Thorne at last.

"Asa?" Beth repeated.

Asa turned to Beth. "I'd really like Xana's take on everything. I trust her intuition. She's uncanny."

"Uncanny at what? What are you talking about? Who are these folks?" she said.

"I went to the City yesterday morning and Xana read my tarot cards," Asa said.

Beth's eyes opened wide. "Get out," she said.

"No, really. What she said caused me to hire Thorne and Don, and they've been on the job since then. I would like Xana's insights into our situation," he said.

"Asa, are you sure? This is all sounding pretty weird," Beth said.

"Something is really wrong here," Asa insisted. "Something dangerous. I just feel it. Please trust that I know what I'm doing."

Everyone waited. The twins stared at each other. Finally Beth nodded. "Oh all right, I'm in," she said.

"Beth, I want to tell them everything and see where that leads us."

"Everything?"

Beth's face bloomed into a blush and she put

her hands to her cheeks to cover it.

"Everything," Asa said. "Please."

The siblings gazed at each other, silent communication passing between them.

"Okay," she said quietly. "Should I stay?"

"If you're willing, I think we could benefit from your point of view."

Beth sighed. She turned the chair next to hers so that the seat faced her, leaned back and put her feet up on the empty seat. She was facing Asa, and facing away from Thorne and Don.

"Okay. You start," she said, resting one arm on the table.

Asa took a deep breath, looked me in the eye, and told me the story. When he stumbled a little, Beth took over. She moved closer to Asa when too many feelings seemed to be ramming through too few psychic pathways, hooking her arm around his shoulders and finishing sentences for him when he stalled, his throat choked shut with emotion.

I was struck by the partnership of it. The thought came to me that Asa worked intuitively, creatively, right-brain-style; Beth seemed to be the implementer, the logician, the practical left-brain element in the pairing. They were more than close siblings. They were mentally and emotionally conjoined.

I admit to being both surprised and not surprised by the facts as subsequently presented. The medical history was a shock, even with Hermes the Magician Card and the associated concept of dual sexuality leading off Asa's card reading.

"Beth and I are twins," he said. "We were born without a specific gender." His voice shook. "We have never told anyone outside the family about this." He looked at Beth.

"When we were born the doctors were unable to decide whether we were genetically female or male," Beth said. "Babies like us used to be called hermaphrodites. We were born before they did tests to figure out what the chromosomes said about a baby's gender. This was back when people were completely freaked out about what was considered a disgraceful deformity. It still is."

"Our parents were stunned," Asa picked up the thread. "I mean it is shocking. What do you announce to your family and friends? Is it a boy or a girl? Neither? Both?" Asa lifted his palms up in a question.

"Nowadays it's a little more common to wait and do tests to see what the child's genetic information says before you do any surgical intervention," Beth took over. "Unless urinary function is restricted, doctors—the more educated ones anyway—mostly recommend waiting before they do anything to establish a specific gender.

"It's really smarter to wait," she went on, "even though it can prove embarrassing and very difficult for parents—for anyone—to provide the diaper changing, bathing, all that personal tending that a baby needs. Back when we were born the doctors took their best guess as to gender and started surgeries right away. My parents did what their doctor recommended." She stopped and looked at Asa.

There was silence. Finally Asa spoke. "They made me a boy and they made Beth a girl." Tears began to slide down his cheeks.

Beth knelt and held Asa's hand as he wept.

"Asa is really my twin sister," she said to us, gently stroking Asa's hair. "We started this company because we believe the technology will enable us to grow the organs we need so we can both be who we really are."

Don fetched a box of tissues from the credenza and handed them to Beth. She pulled two out and gave them to Asa.

"Come on now, Sis," she said as he wiped his face.

Asa blew his nose and looked up at the men.

"You think this is disgusting, I'm sure," he said.

Don looked at Thorne. Thorne nodded for Don to do the talking.

"Unexpected, yes," Don said to Asa. "Disgusting is more like what the doctors did to you when you were too young to make your own decision. I don't think being uncomfortable with somebody else's gender or lack of it gives anybody the right to intervene surgically. I think the Nazis pretty much established the set point on the immorality of human experimentation without permission."

The twins looked at Thorne. Thorne nodded. They looked at me. I nodded.

"I have to admit I'm surprised," Asa said. "This has been such a secret for so long. It makes my family, particularly my father, very uncomfortable, to say the least. You all seem so matter of fact about it and it's been such a weight my family has been struggling under all this time."

"So stop," Thorne said. "If you don't like carrying the weight, drop it. Welcome to adulthood."

Asa and Beth both stared at Thorne. Suddenly Beth laughed, and Asa, with an explosion of raucous and relieved noise, joined her.

"This is what you meant when you were talking about the Tower Card in my reading, wasn't it?" Asa said to me once he stopped laughing.

"You're the only one who can decide that. What's going on that's causing you to think so?"

He opened his mouth to explain but the speaker phone squatting in the middle of the table beeped with an incoming call.

Beth tapped a button and said, "Yes, Elena."

"Your father is in the lobby, Beth, with Sergei and Marcus. He's asking to see you and Asa." As the receptionist spoke we heard a man's angry voice through the speaker, demanding to be let into the offices immediately.

"Tell him where we are, Elena, and let him in please," said Beth, tapping another button to end the call.

"Did you ask him here?" she said to Asa.

"Good God no. We agreed it would not be a good idea." Asa turned to Thorne, a worried frown darkening his face.

Thorne stood up straight, away from where he had been leaning on the wall next to the door. We heard and felt the floor reverberating from multiple sets of footsteps rushing toward us from the direction of the lobby. Suddenly there were three angry-looking men pressing up to the conference room door.

The one in front, a sixty-ish version of Asa and Beth, tried to turn the doorknob, but Thorne had his hand on it first, which meant the contest for doorknob supremacy was never a contest. Thorne's suede work boot was planted against the base of the door as well, blocking it from opening even if by some miracle one of the men outside managed to get the knob to turn.

Don, meanwhile, stretched his arms out to shepherd Asa and Beth to the far side of the table, positioning himself between the twins and the door.

"It's just Dad," Beth protested and took a step from behind Don.

"Stay behind me, please," he said and herded her back.

With Asa's father were, as I learned once we were introduced, Marcus the venture capitalist and Sergei the operations director. Outside the door, the tall, dark-haired and dark-eyed Sergei reached around Asa's father and pounded on the glass with his fist. Thorne put his forearm against the door where Sergei was pounding to support the glass so it would remain intact in spite of the pounding. Marcus, a stout gray-haired man with a bright pink complexion, was standing behind the other two. He looked upset, but he wasn't yelling or pounding.

The two angry men were shouting now, demanding to be let in. Employees were standing up on the chairs in their cubicles, peering out over the high partitions at the disturbance.

"Stop," Thorne said through the glass to Sergei. Thorne didn't seem to be making an effort to be heard, but I could feel the timbre of his voice physically. I couldn't see Thorne's face from where I was sitting, but Sergei looked up at him and his fist froze in place. His face reminded me of one of the children at Marine World watching the tiger pass by.

Asa's father continued ranting, focused on Don and the twins shielded behind Don, until Thorne switched his attention from Sergei and said to him, "Calm down."

Marcus put a pudgy, diamond-ringed hand on Asa's father's shoulder. Turning to shake off

Marcus's hand Asa's dad looked up at Thorne, stopped yelling, and let go of his grip on the doorknob. The three men outside stood there, staring upward at Thorne through the glass, transfixed.

When they had been unmoving and silent for a few more seconds, Thorne opened the door to the men and pointed at three adjacent chairs across the table from the twins and me. The three men walked in, turning to watch Thorne as they did, and sat down. Thorne stood behind the chairs and nodded at Don.

Don stepped aside from the twins and pulled out chairs next to me for Asa and Beth. They sat down. Don stood at one end of the table, between the twins and the three men. Thorne returned to his position leaning against the wall next to the door.

I remained the pattern of all patience, saying nothing.

"What the hell is going on here?" demanded Asa's father, his ferocity rekindled now that he was no longer looking at Thorne but at his off-spring. "Who are these people?" He waved a hand around to indicate Thorne and Don and me. He started to rise, but Thorne was there instantly, gripping the back of the man's chair and pushing the chair into the table, forcing Asa's dad to sit back down.

"Dad, I'd like you to meet some consultants

I've brought on board," Asa said. "I can see you've already met Marcus and Sergei."

He introduced Thorne and Don and me to his father. It turned out Asa's Dad was a doctor too; the elder Dr. Ballantine's first name was Frank.

"I have no interest in meeting any of these people," Dr. Frank said.

"Be still," Thorne said. Ballantine looked up at Thorne and was still.

Marcus stood and reached across the table to shake hands with me, turning around for tacit approval from Thorne before he did so. "Delighted," Marcus said, smiling, taking my hand by the fingertips as if he were about to kiss them, and holding onto them even after I tried to pull them away. I smelled the acrid pong of cigars. Under Marcus's navy blazer he had on a blue shirt that was unbuttoned an alarming number of buttons, revealing gray hair and a mottled and crepe-y chest. I got the disagreeable impression that he expected I would be flattered by his flirtatiousness.

I forced myself to look at Thorne rather than at Marcus and his unwavering eye contact. Unseen by Marcus, Thorne mimed sticking a finger down his throat.

"Asa, what is the deal with these guys?" Sergei asked again, his tone aggressive and unhappy.

"Yes, Asa," said Marcus. "You know you are supposed to discuss any substantive changes in the project plan with me before proceeding. Anything that will have fiscal impact." He crossed his arms over his midriff and looked down his nose at Asa.

"I believe my personal security needs to be enhanced," said Asa. "These gentlemen are the security consultants I will be working with."

"What are you talking about?" Sergei demanded.

"What enhancements?" Marcus spoke at the same time. There was a pause. "And why do you need protecting?" Marcus asked.

"For the time being I'm afraid I have told you all I can," Asa said. "I may be able to provide more information going forward."

"This is unacceptable," Sergei said. "I mean, who are these guys? We're supposed to reach consensus before moving ahead on this kind of decision."

"Or any decisions involving additional financial outlay," Marcus added.

"The costs, for the time being, will be mine alone to bear," Asa said. "And there will be no impact on the project plan."

"What firm do these gentlemen work for?" Sergei asked.

"Mr. Ardall has his own firm," Asa said. "Mr. Madrone is Mr. Ardall's associate."

"Never heard of them. And her?" Sergei said, turning his head toward me.

"Miss Bard is also Mr. Ardall's associate."

There was silence for a few moments.

"I don't understand, Asa," Marcus said.

"Me neither," said Sergei. "And I don't like it. I'm supposed to be in charge of security. You should've talked to me before making a unilateral decision to beef things up with new staff that I haven't had any say in hiring, and who aren't trained on the procedures I've put in place. We've had no chance to do our normal vetting. I have no idea about their capabilities or allegiances."

"I think we can all agree that Sergei has done an exemplary job with security," said Marcus. "I don't see why you feel the need to incur this added expense."

"These three consultants will be working here for the foreseeable future," Asa said firmly. "They may bring in others, which I will approve as necessary, and they will report to me. You need not trouble yourself about them, Sergei, except that they will need all-access twenty-four-hour badges. The paperwork is in process for the badges."

"But where did you find these people?" Sergei said, his voice rising. He raised both arms and dropped them in frustration. He and Marcus turned to look at the two big men.

The two big men said nothing. Don watched Marcus and Sergei. Thorne watched Frank. Asa and Beth looked at each other and said nothing.

"Asa," Frank said, unable to be still any longer, "I absolutely forbid this. You will not spend another minute on this impossible enterprise, this futile quest, and you will lose these money-grubbers and charlatans this instant." He waved his hand in a circle, I assumed to encompass all of us in the room, but especially Don and Thorne and me. His hand brushed against Thorne's shirt.

"Manners," said Thorne from behind the chair, catching and holding Dr. Ballantine's wrist. The doctor tried to yank his arm free; held up that way his hand looked like that of a student who had the answer and was dying to be called on.

Thorne held onto his wrist until Dr. Ballantine stopped trying to yank it away, and then let it go. It was childish, yes, but sometimes Thorne must have his little fun.

"Frank, my dear sir," began Marcus in an oily, lecturing tone. He amended the appellation upon seeing Frank's glare. "Dr. Ballantine. We are quite close to achieving an astounding medical breakthrough. You should be proud of what Asa and Beth have managed to accomplish."

"Do not presume to tell me what I should be proud of." Frank wheeled on Marcus, his face red with fury. "What you are attempting here is an abomination, and it must stop. If you do not suspend this research willingly and immediately, I will do whatever it takes to make it stop. Do you understand me, Asa? Beth?" Frank glared at his grown children.

The twins were upwards of thirty years old, graduates of Stanford Medical School, on the cusp of revolutionary scientific innovation, and he spoke to them as if they were bratty infants throwing a tantrum in a fancy restaurant. Their faces were ashen with shock.

Your parents are your parents no matter how old you are.

"Dr. Ballantine," I found myself saying, forgetting my usual reticence about involving myself in somebody else's family squabble, "You are being very disagreeable, and you are failing to maintain proper perspective."

That's how I roll, people, under the influence of the ripe red poppies.

"You shut the fuck up." He pointed at me, rather venomously I thought. He was definitely snarling, and not with the cool sort of Elvis/Billy Idol snarl that is so sexy and attractive.

Suddenly Dr. Ballantine was upright, swept away to the conference room door. Before anyone realized it was happening, Thorne had hoisted him out of his chair, opened the conference room door, and propelled him out into the lobby.

We heard Dr. Ballantine yelling, *"Hey! Hey!"* and then the yelling was muffled by the closing lobby doors and Thorne was back in the conference room, leaning serenely against the wall.

We were all quiet for a minute.

"Well," Beth said. "That was awful." To

Thorne she said, "You, however, are awesome."

Thorne smiled slightly. Thorne is completely aware that he is awesome, but I guess he enjoys having it affirmed by others now and again. He resembles actual humans in that way.

The speaker phone rang. Asa reached it and pressed a button. "Hold all calls please, Elena," he said over the sound of his father's loud voice in the speaker. "Thank you." He pressed a button and the sound stopped.

Asa turned to Beth and said, "How the hell did Dad find out?"

"Not me," she said, shaking her head at him. "You know I wouldn't. I told him tissue regeneration, not organ regeneration. As far as I know he thought we were working on growing skin for burn victims."

They looked at Marcus and Sergei. Marcus swallowed and turned pinker than he already was. He cleared his throat.

"Marcus?" Beth said.

"Beth, I spoke your father after our earlier meeting because he had called and left a message inquiring about participation in the financial underwriting of the project. I did not realize that he was unaware of the exact nature of our research. I mean, really; how could you not have told him? He's your father and a prominent medical man himself. His influence will be far-reaching when it comes time for testing and approval of our products. I could tell he was astounded, very impressed by what I told him."

"Marcus, you should never have revealed the specifics of our project," Asa said. "You could not possibly understand the ramifications of his learning what we are researching here."

"Asa and Beth, I am entitled as the venture capitalist funding the enterprise to avail myself of any reasonable resource as long as it does not infringe on the agreed-upon equity distribution of the company."

"Hang on a minute," said Sergei. "You were going to ask him to buy in?"

"Not necessarily. Not without discussion among the partners. It was an exploratory conversation only. But developments are moving more slowly than originally anticipated. I felt it was appropriate to seek possible alternative sources of capital."

"He would have demanded equity," Sergei said. "You know he would. So get this straight, Marcus. There's no way I am diluting my shares by adding new partners. If you are running out of money we are entitled to know that." Sergei was raising his voice. Don and Thorne moved to flank the men, monitoring whether the argument was spiraling up into more than mere noise.

"It's not even that," Asa said. "What's most important is that Dad will find a way to abort the project. He meant it when he threatened to stop us. Marcus is right that Dad is wired into everyone everywhere, for God's sake. He'll call in every chip he's got out there. You have no idea what you've set in motion."

"Oh I doubt that very much," said Marcus smugly. "After all, when we are successful there will be tremendous financial returns for everyone involved. He has to see the benefit to himself, to the two of you. To his reputation by proxy. To humanity," he added as an afterthought.

"Marcus," Beth said. She had collected herself, sitting upright with her arms folded across each other on the table. She was poised, clear, formal.

"You have been very good to us," she said, "getting us up on our feet with this company. Nevertheless you have made a dreadful error informing an outsider, albeit our Dad, about what we are researching here. A dreadful error," she repeated.

Asa?" she said, turning to her brother, "we need to regroup and consider this development, yes?"

"We do," he said, turning to Marcus and Sergei. "I need your assurance that neither of you will speak to my father again or to anyone else about this until Beth and I have had a chance to discuss our next steps."

"Don't look at me," Sergei said. "I'm not the one who let the cat out of the bag, and I'm starting to feel like I'm the last one to find out anything around here. As an equity partner I should be involved in any decisions that affect the progress or outcomes of the project, and suddenly I am the last one finding out anything."

"Give us one day, please, Sergei," Beth said.

Sergei shook his head no, but said, "All right. One day. But we meet first thing the day after tomorrow to agree as a team on how to proceed. No unilateral decisions from now on."

"Excellent," Beth said. She turned to Marcus. "And you?"

"If it is your wish that I suspend inquiries with your father and others about capital funding options, certainly I will comply." Marcus bowed his head and smiled carefully.

"Are there others you've contacted? Others you've told about the research?"

"Not at this point in time."

"Good."

My guess was that Marcus, on whose forehead small beads of sweat were now glistening, had not bothered to have the senior Dr. Ballantine sign a non-disclosure agreement. It was a major gaffe, the outcome of which might well be lawsuits flung at Marcus up and down the Peninsula. He had heard the distant thunder of process server footsteps in Beth's tone.

"Sergei, shall we chat about this over a little something?" Marcus said. "It's getting to be that time of day."

I know from little somethings. Mater mixes herself one or two or three little somethings every afternoon. From the pinkness of Marcus's complexion, especially his nose, I thought the little somethings were likely to be a sacred daily ritual.

"Sure," said Sergei. "I could use a drink. I'll talk to you both tomorrow," he said, turning to Beth and Asa. "We need to settle the issue of these consultants. I don't want to wait until the day after tomorrow for that discussion."

"Fine," Asa said. "I'll be in early."

When the men had left Asa turned to me. "Xana? Thoughts?"

"Well," I said, trying not to sound like Jack Benny. "An interesting set of players." I was matching the three men up with what I had visualized while reading Asa's cards. His Dad was the man I had seen in the white hallway with the red-haired woman. A younger version, but definitely Asa's and Beth's Dad.

"Yes," Asa said. "What's your take on Marcus and Sergei? And on my Dad too, if you can."

I thought about it. "Some of what's happening is obvious enough. Marcus is cash-strapped. Also, I would avoid leaving him alone in private with any of your female employees. Three open buttons on his shirt is not a good look for him, but he thinks it's sexy when his behavior is in fact really creepy. Sergei is banking heavily on a financial payoff when you get FDA approval. Your Dad understands where the research is headed within his family and hates the idea."

"But why?" Beth said, exasperated. "Why should he care? We've argued about Asa's wanting to have surgery within the family, but really, it has nothing to do with Dad. And this research will help everyone in the world. It couldn't be more important."

She put her arm around Asa. I sat still and waited for something to occur to me.

"He is much angrier than seems appropriate. In my experience, when people are that angry they have a problem with forgiveness. Not forgiving others so much as forgiving themselves. They blame themselves for having allowed something to happen that they now realize was wrong, or self-destructive, or just stupid. And it makes them furious, because there's nothing they can do about it now. So they aim their fury everywhere—especially at the people they've harmed by their actions. Aiming their fury at themselves is too painful, so they blame the people who triggered their stupidity."

Beth and Asa looked at each other. She put her hand on his and squeezed.

"What standing does your father have in the medical community?" I asked. "How is he viewed by his peers? How much does he care about that?"

"He's a very prominent and highly-regarded

neurosurgeon," Beth said. "He's the go-to-guy for cranial aneurisms and cancers in the Western United States. He speaks at major conferences worldwide. He finds a way to introduce his exalted position into every conversation."

"My take on him matches that information. This is just my impression, okay? This is not necessarily the actuality of what is going on. I've only seen the man for a few minutes, under circumstances that were obviously very stressful for him."

"I hear all the caveats," Asa said. "Just say it."

"I think he's mortified. I think he's afraid people will find out what happened when the two of you were born. He thinks it will reflect badly on him. And I think the realization that he made a mistake with Asa has thrown him into a panic."

I had spoken as I did when I was reading cards, without consciously putting the words into a rational sequence.

Asa and Beth stared at me.

"But that makes no sense," Asa said. "Birth defects can happen to anyone. It wasn't his fault."

"I don't think we saw a rational response from him this afternoon. Do you?"

"Asa, we were afraid of this," Beth said. "It's why we never told him what we were really doing." She spoke quietly, leaning toward her twin.

We were all quiet, watching the twins communicate silently.

"It's getting late," Beth said finally, patting Asa on the arm. "Let's sleep on this and get together again tomorrow."

Asa sat with his head down on the table, resting on his crossed arms. "Okay," he said into his arms.

Beth stood and walked behind my chair along the vertical blinds blocking the view of the world outside. She reached the end of the glass wall closest to Thorne and lifted the panels to look out into the dusk-dimmed landscape as Thorne and Don both said, "*No!*" and moved to stop her.

They were too late.

The glass splintered, with a sound like thin ice cracking on a frozen pond, and there was a thwap of something solid hitting something not so solid.

Beth said "*Hunh,*" spun to her left, and fell sideways into Thorne's arms.

The released vertical blind swung back across the spider-web cracks in the plate glass, the cracks radiating from a small jagged hole.

Don shoved Asa to the floor, yanked my chair away from the table, pulled me roughly down next to Asa and shielded us from the curtained glass with his body. My cast clunked onto the floor and my theretofore quiet ankle flashed with a massive pang. Don reached into a holster inside his jacket, pulled out a gun and aimed it at the glass.

Asa screamed.

≈18≈

Agatha sat in her sunny kitchen and checked her list.

- ~~Bedding~~
- ~~Mattress~~
- Bullets
- ~~Box spring?~~
- ~~Call R's office~~
- ~~Headboard?~~
- ~~Plaster?~~
- ~~R & L bag/bury?~~
- ~~Bank~~
- ~~Paint?~~
- ~~Fabric~~
- Pistol
- ~~Linda clothing/car?~~
- ~~Vacuuming~~

She analyzed the only remaining tasks: Bullets and Pistol.

With a start she realized that all she needed to dispose of was the bullets and casings. Since she had found them all while cleaning up, and they were the only way to trace the use of the pistol, she could clean and replace the gun in its locked cabinet and throw the bullets and casings away. All the clothing she had worn during what she now called "the housekeeping" she had washed and dropped off at Goodwill on Mission Street.

She went to her bedroom and picked up the eight pieces of metal from Rolf's coin tray. Putting on her raincoat, she slipped them into her pocket and walked downstairs and across the street to Sutro Park.

The nasturtiums lining the paths bloomed yellow and orange against the round green leaves. Agatha inhaled the fragrance of the eucalyptus trees and leaned her head back to watch their silvery leaves rustling in the breeze off the ocean.

The dog walkers were all at work by now; there was no one else in the small park. She stopped at a nasturtium bed and bent over as if to touch one of the blooms. A bullet slid off her fingers into the dirt. She pressed it into the soil and stood.

Agatha continued her stroll around the park, watching for anyone who might observe her, and seven more times bent to examine a nasturtium and bury evidence.

She stood at the western edge of the park and gazed out over the Pacific. The water was dark blue today, with smooth waves rolling onto the shore. The surfers would be out, she thought, jogging unshod in their wetsuits across the Great Highway, lugging their boards under their arms as they hurried to the water.

Agatha thought of how peaceful that must be, to sit on the board as the low waves swept under you, to rise and fall on the water, to wait patiently for the one wave that would give you the perfect ride. But she also knew that in the water you ran the risk of encountering great white sharks and rogue waves.

She realized that her life stretched ahead of her now, limitless like the ocean, and she felt unafraid. Rolf had been the rogue wave in her life and she had survived the buffeting he had forced her to endure.

Agatha turned to head home. She would have to think carefully about what her next steps would be once she had cleaned and shelved the pistol, once her house was truly in order.

She would find out where the rest of Rolf's money and investments were kept. Her money, her investments now. She would decide how soon to call the police and report her husband missing. She would think about the right way to behave with the police. What story should she tell?

She thought it best to leave the girlfriend aspect up to others to mention; she felt it would be unwise to acknowledge that she knew anything about Rolf's shenanigans with Linda. She would express dismay and astonishment at Rolf's disappearance. She would be the dim-witted *hausfrau* for the police. She knew how to enact that role to perfection. She would have to practice crying, though. She wasn't sure she could muster any tears for Rolf. Definitely not for Linda.

What should she do about the real estate business? What legal expertise would she require in order to take charge of Rolf's business and financial affairs?

Most important right now, where should she go to buy new clothes? To get her hair done properly? To learn about cosmetics and manicures? She was a new woman. She wanted to look the part.

She needed to buy the clothes that a wealthy, respected woman would wear, not the dowdy, shapeless, homemade things worn by a big-boned middle-aged German farm girl, an abused servant indentured to a heartless taskmaster. She needed to adopt and perfect the grooming of a rich woman who pampered herself.

Back in the house she changed clothes, putting on a dark red dress she had only worn once, to a Christmas party at Rolf's real estate firm. She felt feminine in the dress, a sensation that was almost unknown to her in her former life with Rolf.

She looked in the mirror and assessed herself. Her figure was not voluptuous. She was sturdy, not overweight, square-shouldered and strong. Her hair was drab and graying and pulled back into a low ponytail. Her hands were red-knuckled from cooking and scrubbing.

She would go to one of the expensive hair-dressers downtown and see about a new color and style instead of the simple page boy she had trimmed herself all these years. She would go to a nail salon and have her work-roughened hands and feet attended to. She would get a facial and learn how to use cosmetics and moisturizers so that her drab skin would glow and her pale blue eyes would light up.

She pulled the skin on her forehead upward and saw the worry lines flatten; perhaps a plastic surgeon could help her recover some lost years.

The phone rang. She hesitated, then walked to the nightstand and answered it.

"Mrs. Hein, it's Betsy from the office," the young voice said.

"Yes dear?"

"I'm calling to see if you've heard from Mr. Hein."

"No, I have not heard."

Nor will I, she thought. *Nor will you. Nor will anybody.*

"He was scheduled to meet with clients yesterday and today, but he hasn't come in and we haven't heard from him. We thought he might have checked in with you."

"Have you tried calling his cell phone?"

"Yes, of course."

Agatha heard condescension in Betsy's tone.

"It's going straight to voice mail," Betsy said.

"Well, then, I have no idea what to recommend. All Linda told me was that he was going out of town for a few days on business."

"Yes, but the prospects in Massachusetts say they haven't heard from him either."

Agatha said nothing for a moment. "Do you know what flight he took? Has there been any sort of accident that you know of that he might have been involved in?"

"There's been nothing like that, Mrs. Hein. We were hoping you'd know more than we do here at the office, especially since his assistant is also not in today. We can't reach her either."

"Was she planning to go on the trip with him?" Agatha smiled grimly to herself. *Let this silly child respond to that*, she thought.

"I don't know, Mrs. Hein. I don't think so."

There was silence.

"Well, I am not sure what I can do," Agatha said. "All I know is he was traveling for a few days. He does not ever give me any details."

"Okay." Betsy paused. "I'll ask the other

agents what they want to do about today's clients. But this is unlike Mr. Hein, to have this kind of mix-up, to not be in touch."

"Do you think I should notify someone? Should I call the police?" Agatha tried to sound helplessly incapable of making such a decision on her own.

"Let me check with the senior agent. I'll call you back if we hear anything. I'm sorry if I've scared you."

"All right. I will call also if I hear anything. Let us talk tomorrow morning in any case, and decide what to do then."

"Certainly, Mrs. Hein. Take care."

Hanging up the phone, Agatha thought she already taken care. Very good care.

"I will make a return trip to the Twins' Armoire after all. There is still plenty of time this afternoon. Perhaps I will go to Union Square to the big stores. Tomorrow I will see about the new hairdo and the manicure. I want to give my new appearance an entire day. A day of luxury."

She went to the closet to change into one of her cotton dresses and put on her good shoes.

≈19≈

Thorne lifted Beth and carried her to the door of the conference room. He pressed the light switch and the room went dark.

"Asa," Thorne said. "Come. Don, the parking lot."

"Stay down," Don said to me. "Don't open the blinds."

"Just go," I said. "Go go go go."

Don, placing himself between Asa and the bullet-pierced glass wall, rushed Asa out of the conference room on Thorne's heels. Voices were raised out in the cubicles.

On my hands and knees, my left leg bent to hold my left foot and the heavy cast up off the floor, I crawled under the table and out the conference room door to the tall cubicles across the aisle. Inside the first empty one I put both fore-arms flat onto the desk surface, set my good foot on the floor and pressed myself upright onto my right leg.

I sat down in the desk chair and turned so my feet were under the work surface. One of the lab-coated employees walked up and stood in the doorway looking anxious.

"What just happened?" she said.

"You should not stand there," I said, turning slightly toward her but still hiding my left leg under the desktop. I reached toward her and pulled on the sleeve of her lab coat. "Come inside here with me." She stepped into the cubicle and side-ways out of the entryway.

"Has anyone called 911 yet?" I asked her.

"Yes. I was in the lobby and I heard the big man who was carrying Beth tell Elena to call. He said they were going to Stanford. Then the other big guy came in from outside and said it was clear and they all ran out the door. But what on earth happened to Beth? She was bleeding and Asa was pressing his hand on her as they were running."

"Please ask everyone to stay here in the build-ing away from the windows until the police ar-rive? There was a gunshot through the conference room window. Beth was hurt."

"Oh my God, is she okay?"

I know this is the sort of thing people say un-der the circumstances, but even so. Not to mention I had not entirely sobered up yet, so the look I gave the woman was untempered.

"Right, right, of course," she said. "She's not okay. Oh God. I see. But meanwhile, who are all you people and what are you doing here?"

"Please. That can wait. Let's keep everyone safe for now. Don't say anything about Beth being hurt yet."

"You're right. Okay. I'll tell Elena to make an announcement to stay away from the windows." She bent over and scuttled down the aisle toward the lobby.

"Tell Elena to come away from the lobby as well," I shouted.

"Okay."

The fact is, shootings in Bay Area buildings are not unheard of. Over the years there have been multiple murderous occurrences.

Welcome to America, all you huddled masses. Here's your complimentary handgun.

The announcement to stay away from the windows came over the ceiling speakers. People in the big work space gathered in cubicles at the center of the room and whispered.

I heard sirens approaching. If the shooter was still outside, which was highly unlikely, he or she would take off now.

I rolled myself, propelling the chair backward with my right foot, into the dark conference room. I grabbed my purse, jacket, sofa cushion, crutches, and ice bags. I did not want these to be gathered up in the evidence dragnet. I rolled down the aisle to a different cubicle, closer to the lobby.

The sirens were nearer. I thought about what was likely to happen if I remained in the cubicle. I rolled myself as fast as I could out to and across the lobby to the ladies room I had spotted there when I arrived.

Elena was no longer at the reception console. I don't believe anyone saw me.

Flashing lights strobed the lobby walls as I turned the chair frontwards and pulled the rest room door open. I rolled in and pulled the rest room door shut again. I turned off the light switch next to the door and the room went black. I used the flashlight app on my cell phone to light my way into the handicapped stall.

I debated whether to shut the stall door and decided against it. If someone were to turn on the light to look, let them think the open stall doors meant the restroom was vacant. If someone came in to use the rest room, I could shut the stall door then.

I also debated whether to elevate my leg by resting it on the toilet. There was no seat cover to pull down. But my leg was in a cast, after all, and I would not be touching the seat with my skin. I could pull down and unfold a tissue paper seat cover...

No. I remembered my cast slipping off the

wheelchair's foot rest.

Time passed. I heard the police moving back and forth through the lobby, their voices raised, their radios squawking. No one looked for me in the rest room, which surprised me. I was sure the woman who had spoken to me in the cubicle would say something and they would search for me.

I was the pattern of all patience. I opened a Tracy Chevalier novel on my phone, rested the phone on the sofa cushion in my lap, and read about ammonites and Lyme Regis. Time passed. The noises from the lobby became intermittent.

My ankle throbbed. I opened the stall door and scooped water from the sink spigot into my hand, swallowing a half tab of Oxy. My ankle continued to throb, but the Oxy kicked in and I stopped caring.

I sent a text to Thorne: ?

I received a reply within two minutes: *OMW.* On my way.

Fuzz. I'm hiding.

RTG?

I hope you are not driving and texting. Yes, ready to go.

Exit bldg south end 5 mins.

K I sent, and started to pack up.

I put my phone in my purse. I zipped the sofa cushion up inside my jacket, folded the jacket over so the bottom end was up instead of down, and tied the arms around my waist so that I was carrying the pillow like a baby in a sling.

I emptied the now watery ice into the sink and stuffed the empty plastic bags into the trash bin. I changed my mind and lifted the bags back out and put them in my purse. I slung the long strap of the purse over my head and under my left arm, the strap across my chest holding the pillow-stuffed jacket in place. I wriggled my hands into the gloves Thorne had given me.

I rolled backwards to the rest room door, feeling my way in the dark, and listened. The lobby was quiet. I pushed the door open a crack and peeked. The lobby was empty. I stood up on the crutches and pushed the desk chair away.

I shoved the rest room door open wide and planted a rubber crutch tip against the bottom edge to hold the door open. I swung out around the door and to the left, pulling the propped crutch out of the way so the door could shut behind me. I hopped toward the end of the hall fifteen feet away, where an exit sign's green letters glowed above the solid metal door. I turned myself around and shoved against the door's hip-height push bar to open it. I almost lost my balance as the door was pulled away from me. I felt a frying-pan-sized hand against my back, steadying me.

"Crutches," Thorne said. I handed them to him and he tucked them under his arm. I balanced on my right foot, but that was easy enough to do with Thorne holding me steady. I untied my jacket from around my waist and the sofa cushion fell out. Thorne caught it.

I slipped on my jacket over my purse. Thorne handed the cushion to me and up I went into his arms. He held the crutches alongside me in both hands like a crib rail.

"What do you know about Beth?" I whispered as he carried me away quickly and quietly from the building.

"Not good."

"But not dead?

"Not dead. Surgery."

"Did you find the shooter?"

"No."

"Is Don staying with Asa at the hospital?"

"Yes."

"Why aren't the police watching that door?"

We were almost to his car, parked in the lot behind the next building in the business park.

"I don't know."

"Are they letting other people leave the building?"

"I didn't see."

"Where are we going from here?"

"To Bonebreak," Thorne said.

Bix Bonebreak runs a steel fabricating plant, among other overt as well as more mysterious enterprises. Thorne and I had met him in the course of finding a killer. Bix, who struck me as a decent enough man, if more than slightly rough-hewn, had been uninvolved in the murder.

He had nevertheless not hesitated to buy the murdered man's company from the grieving widow as soon as the funeral director carted away the floral arrangements.

Thorne was driving fast up Highway 101 toward the City, where Bonebreak's factory was.

"Why Bonebreak?"

"More muscle. More eyes."

"Will he help you?"

"Yes."

"Why?"

Thorne didn't answer.

"Is there some sort of badass mutual aid society?"

Thorne didn't answer.

Guarding Asa had begun as a precaution and turned into a job that was suddenly violence-marred, if not deadly. Thorne would ask Bix to loan him some bruisers who were familiar with averting damage to some humans and inflicting damage on others.

As Mater would say, Bix "has people who do that sort of thing."

≈20≈

Agatha sat in her lamp-lit living room surrounded by shopping bags full of her purchases. She
had found the sister Twins in their Armoire this
time. The two eccentric women outfitted her in
wonderful, glamorous clothes, things she would
never have dreamed of wearing before.

She bought everything they put on her, using
Rolf's card. The Twins recommended a hairdresser and even made a call for her, arranging an appointment for tomorrow; they knew the hairdresser and could call in a favor. Agatha felt for-
tunate to know people who had such influence.

She'd been afraid the Twins would ask about
her sudden shopping and makeover whirlwind,
but she need not have worried. The Twins focused on high-fashion outfits that suited Agatha's

coloring and physique, asking no personal questions. She loved everything, but realized she would need a more tailored and subdued wardrobe for everyday wear.

She had been afraid the bank would halt her buying mid-spree. Before leaving the house she called the toll-free number listed in tiny white print on the back of Rolf's card and, after pressing many keys, reached a person instead of the recorded messages.

She explained to the man who called himself Doug, although she thought his name was more likely to be Rajhnish, that she would be making some major purchases over the next few days and wanted to alert the bank in advance. Doug thanked her for calling and said he would provide immediate and excellent service and would make a note in the account.

From the Twins' Armoire Agatha drove down Nob Hill to Union Square and parked in the underground garage. She walked into Saks Fifth Avenue and wandered through the floors looking at the racks of clothing. She had no idea what to try on.

A saleswoman approached her. "May I help you find something?" Agatha noticed the saleswoman looking her up and down, taking in her home-sewn cotton dress, her plain shoes.

"I need a new wardrobe," Agatha said carefully. She was not sure whether the word was correct. Did "wardrobe" mean a piece of furniture or the clothing that went into the piece of furniture? The saleswoman introduced herself as Lorraine and seemed to understand what Agatha meant, so "wardrobe" must have been the proper word.

"Where will you be wearing your new clothing?" Lorraine asked.

Agatha had to think about that. "To work, and to the symphony and ballet," she finally said.

"What kind of work do you do?"

"Real estate."

That was all Lorraine needed to know, apparently, because she escorted Agatha to a department across the sales floor and began showing her things, asking what Agatha liked and didn't like. Agatha was attracted to simple designs; nothing with a lot of pattern or decoration.

Lorraine did not ask about Agatha's budget, nor did she ever show Agatha any price tags, and it was a strain for Agatha not to grab the tags and read for herself what she was certain must be shocking prices.

Lorraine asked Agatha's size and began pulling garments off the racks as they walked through the departments. She took Agatha to a large fitting room and told her she would return shortly. For the next hour Lorraine ferried in and out a series of elegant tailored suits and scarves, silk and cotton blend blouses with muted swirls of color, narrow leather belts with hidden clasps, dresses with clever tailoring that made Agatha feel feminine and attractive.

As she tried on the clothes she watched Lorraine's face to read the saleswoman's assessment of how she looked. After half a dozen changes of clothing Agatha began to see what merited Lorraine's nodding approval and why. The clothes must fit in the shoulders and hips; everywhere else they could be tailored.

Agatha learned that colors needed to suit her skin tone and eyes and hair. The waistline on pants and skirts should sit slightly lower than her waist, to lengthen her short upper body and show off her trim build.

"My shape is not so normal, I think," Agatha apologized.

"My dear, everyone needs to tailor ready-to-wear clothing to get a proper fit. You are slim and tall and you have obviously taken very good care of yourself."

Agatha thought to herself that only in the last three days had she finally taken care of herself. Before that she had simply worked like a slave.

One navy pantsuit fit like it had been made for her. A pair of black lined wool slacks needed tailoring, and Agatha stood straight in the dressing room as the seamstress pulled seams snug and pinned them. She felt the subtle, impersonal touch of the seamstress through the fabric. She realized that today was the first time in many months that she had been touched by another human being. She wondered if she would ever be caressed, instead of touched with the disinterest of seamstresses, tailors, dentists, hairdressers.

When Lorraine asked what shoes she would wear with the pantsuit and slacks in order for the seamstress to adjust the cuff on the slacks, Agatha had not known what to answer. "Nothing with too high a heel," she finally said.

The saleswoman asked her shoe size, disappeared for a few minutes, and brought her two different pairs of black ankle-high boots to try on there in the dressing room. Agatha chose the suede ones; the soft leather did not press against her bunions.

Lorraine asked, "What jewelry are you planning to wear?"

"I would like your help choosing what would be best."

"I'll bring you some options and we can see what works."

She returned ten minutes later carrying a heavy gold chain necklace and matching bracelet, a multi-strand gleaming gray coin pearl necklace that would sit close to her neckline, a pair of white gold earrings, and a watch with a black face and black leather band. Agatha thought they were all perfect.

Lorraine, ringing up the many purchases,

asked if Agatha would like the clothes hangers, and Agatha realized she would need them. Her few housedresses and pants took up almost no room in the closet and she had no extra hangers. She could not throw out Rolf's clothes yet, so she could not commandeer his hangers.

She turned to go, and then asked if she could change into one of the outfits she had bought. Lorraine snipped the tags off the navy pantsuit and, after Agatha had changed clothes, folded her old dress and shoes into their own shopping bag. Lorraine called for an assistant to help Agatha carry the many bags out of the store into the late afternoon dusk, and then across the street to her car. Agatha tipped the young man twenty dollars.

She came up to the street level again. The sun had set; fog was blowing in across the sky above her; Union Square was windy and chilly.

I need a new coat, Agatha thought. And then she was elated, the way every San Franciscan is elated, to see Marian and Vivian Brown, the San Francisco twins who dress alike and are always together, walking up Post Street. It was rare to see them out and about nowadays, perfectly matched in their wonderfully bright outfits, teased blonde hair, and hats.

Today they had on matching dainty cowboy hats and faux leopard fur jackets, under which they wore red pantsuits. Tourists were stopping them to take their picture, as always. Marian and

Vivian smiled their lovely smiles and, arm in arm, headed toward Agatha at the corner.

Agatha walked across Union Square and crossed Stockton Street into Neiman Marcus, coming out an hour later with more purchases, and wearing a camel hair coat and a white pashmina scarf.

She loaded the shopping bags into the now crowded car trunk and drove to the Mission Street parking garage. It was only a few blocks, but she was not sure how much she would be buying at San Francisco Centre and she did not want to be overburdened walking back up to Union Square.

She obviously needed new shoes and shoes were heavy; she had not thought about shoes, and Nordstrom was the place for shoes. From Nordstrom she would take a quick scouting expedition through Bloomingdales.

The downtown stores stayed open until nine o'clock every day except on weekends, a wonderful convenience. She had bought flamboyant outfits at the Twins' Armoire, but Agatha's Union Square selections she considered practical so far; after all, she was a practical person. Wardrobe-builders, Lorraine at Saks had called the jackets and slacks and dresses. Agatha could wear these clothes for years; they would not go out of style.

After buying twelve pairs of shoes and three handbags at Nordstrom and dropping them off in her car, she found herself unable to resist a deep violet pantsuit at Bloomingdales. With a dark blue and violet knit silk tee under the jacket she saw herself for the first time as a woman who was stylish, not frumpy.

She had forgotten about underwear until she tried on a black wool jersey dress and her white bra showed at the neckline. She spent a few hundred dollars on new lingerie in every color except white.

She put the last of her purchases into the car and walked to Bush Street, to Le Centrale, just downhill from the Chinatown Gate, for dinner. She was hungry and she felt like she was at home in Europe along the banquette, being served salad with a mustard vinaigrette and *cassoulet* by the French-speaking staff. She drank a glass of red Côtes du Rhône and listened to the chatter of the diners on either side of her along the wall. She felt she fit in with the other well-dressed people in the elegant restaurant.

Agatha recognized the liberating release she had felt as she went from store to store, handing over Rolf's card to pay for the expensive clothes he would never have permitted her to buy. She marveled at the experience of being treated so respectfully, so courteously by everyone she dealt with. Even more wonderful was being touched, petted, made a fuss over and told she looked attractive.

In the dressing rooms trying on new clothes Agatha had felt different. No matter what the salespeople told her, she did not feel beautiful. Not yet. But sitting at home in her living room, surrounded by a sea of shopping bags, pulling out garments and reliving the joy of the long afternoon and evening she had spent squandering Rolf's money, she realized that what she felt now was powerful.

She gazed out the picture window at the darkened park across the street. A neighbor was walking his dog. The little dog was so happy, cavorting and jumping up playfully. It was obvious that the dog loved the man.

Agatha wondered if she even knew how to love anyone anymore. And then it came to her that she could begin by loving a pet. With Rolf gone, she could fill the house with animals she could spoil with affection, animals that would love her unconditionally. Warm, friendly animals that would snuggle with her and yearn for her to pet their soft fur.

She would start a new list in the morning.

≈21≈

Beth was recovering at Stanford Hospital. She and Asa were being watched over by Don and two of Bix Bonebreak's muscle-bound, bad-suit-wearing minions, whom Thorne had recruited with Mr. Bonebreak's apparent blessing. The men were taking shifts.

Thorne dropped me at the house after seeing Bonebreak. He changed out of his bloody clothes and packed a bag, and now was gone again down the Peninsula, likely to be gone for some time, on full-time guard duty with Asa and Beth.

Thorne had said almost nothing to me driving back to the City. He seemed more intense than usual, if such a thing were possible. I believe he was furious, given the circumstances, but Thorne elated and Thorne furious can be difficult to distinguish, one from the other.

I was glad for the dulling impact of the drugs I was taking; I know they muted the recurring vision of Beth falling backward and the cracking sound of the glass.

I let out the dogs and fed them, and put kibble into the cat dish on top of the refrigerator. If you have ever owned dogs and cats together, you will understand why the cat food was on top of the refrigerator.

I was sitting in the command post chair, my ankle elevated and iced. I was spooning into myself a small bowlful of Yolanda's superb macaroni and cheese; she had left it on the doorstep when she found me not at home. The appetite suppression effect of the Oxycodone was evident or I would have nuked a tubful of the luscious stuff and scarfed it all down at one sitting.

I was watching a Poirot mystery on PBS that I had seen before, but couldn't remember the denouement of. That's the wonderful thing about Agatha Christie; the murderer is always a surprise, given the impossible irrelevance of every clue Ms. Christie strews across the reader's path during the story.

A blue feather is found under the couch by the housekeeper, which means to Hercule and no one else that the killer must be, *et violà*, the owner of the parakeet, with the murderer's motive generally involving the inability to get a divorce or some other archaic and vaguely aristocratic lunacy.

But Agatha Christie's characters are wonderfully drawn, beautifully observed, and they speak thoroughly entrancing dialogue. Another fascinating element of her mysteries was her encyclopedic knowledge of poisons, picked up when she worked in a pharmacy during the Great War.

I was musing—why not?—about the rarity of poisoning in modern mysteries when across the street the Hein's Mercedes turned into her driveway, Mrs. Hein at the wheel. I mused on the fact that Agatha was both a British and German name.

I wondered where Mr. Hein had gone to. I couldn't recall ever seeing his wife drive the car so frequently. I hoped everything was okay over there.

After a few minutes the living room light came on at the Hein house. That was odd too; I couldn't remember seeing the living room light on in that house before. But then I had not until recently been parked at the front window staring out for hours on end, with nothing to notice but the neighboring houses' lighting patterns.

Through the uncurtained window I saw Mrs. Hein setting down on the floor a crowd of shopping bags: Nordstrom silver, Bloomingdales brown, black and white from Saks, and many others.

She disappeared and returned with more bags; by the time she sat down in the middle of them there were at least twenty large bags surrounding her.

I had never seen Agatha Hein wear anything but the simplest clothes, mostly cotton shirtwaists that looked homemade, or tan slacks and sweaters, with low-heeled shoes made for walking back and forth to the Geary bus parked at the corner.

Tonight she had on a navy suit and black boots, and she had been on a world-class shopping spree.

Good for her.

Tomorrow I would see the orthopedic surgeon and find out when and how my ankle was going to be cobbled back together.

I fell asleep.

I awoke to hear the racket of the crutches falling to the ground at the bottom of the stairs, followed by the scrambling of the cats for someplace low and dark.

I fell asleep again.

I missed Hercule's revelation of the parakeet-owning murderer, or whoever.

I woke up in the middle of the night to a row of dark houses across the street.

I refilled the ice bags, set the alarm in my cell phone, and moved to the sofa to sleep the rest of the night away.

≈22≈

Agatha walked out of the salon on Maiden Lane and turned toward Union Square. She had allowed the hairdresser to dye her graying, mousy hair a dark chestnut color and cut it into a soft precise cap that framed her face. He had shown her how to comb it forward or away from her face and use hair products to hold the style.

The salon housed a day spa, where she underwent her first facial, manicure and pedicure. At another cosmetician's station she learned how to apply makeup. She thought she looked ten years younger. Everyone in the salon had said so, and she believed them.

The manicurist had exclaimed over the state of her hands. "I have been doing a lot of gardening," Agatha said, luxuriating in the feel of the heated lotion the woman was rubbing into her skin.

Walking up Maiden Lane past the Chanel store, Agatha caught sight of herself without recognizing who she was seeing in the shop window. After that she looked in every store window at her reflection. Could she really be this striking woman?

She stopped at Café Mocca for lunch, eating a salad and fruit tart outside at a table under one of the patio umbrellas, listening to the street musicians playing subdued jazz. When the saxophone player came around holding out a hat after a few songs, she put in five dollars and thanked him.

Her new life had begun, and she felt ready for it now. She decided to defer any plastic surgery until she felt more at home in her new appearance. *Take it slowly at first*, she thought. She would go home and shower, to rinse off the irritating snippets of hair that had slipped down her back. After that she would decide what to do next with another lovely unfettered day.

ב ב ב

Agatha came up the stairs at her house to hear the phone ringing. *Ach, I have forgotten about the office. That will be the young Betsy.*

"Hello," Agatha said, out of breath from rushing up the stairs to catch the phone.

"Hello, Mrs. Hein," said a man's voice she did not recognize. "This is Phil Agostino at the real estate office. Is Mr. Hein there, please?"

Agatha felt a rush of alarm. "No, I have not heard from Rolf still."

"Nor have we, and we are getting very concerned. I don't want to worry you, but I think it's very unusual for Mr. Hein to be unavailable for so long. Perhaps we should discuss what our next steps should be, under the circumstances."

Agatha could hear how carefully this Mr. Agostino had rehearsed his speech. He had avoided using inflammatory language; he was skirting the "disappeared" word because he was talking to The Wife, and she was certain he knew about Rolf and Linda.

"What do you recommend?" Agatha said. "I am not familiar with the correct way to proceed. I am worried too, you know. He usually calls me when he is away and I have heard nothing."

Rolf never called her when he was away; she hoped Phil would not know she had just lied. She hoped her voice had conveyed the right amount of emotion, the right type of emotion.

"He has been missing since Monday, Mrs. Hein. I recommend you report this to the San Francisco police and let them pursue it. I don't think I can make a report here that they would investigate. It should come from you."

"All right then. I will make a call."

She wanted to sound tentative, but not like a fool. She would have to play this carefully, as if she were exhibiting lack of familiarity with American procedures rather than stupidity or, worse, awareness of what had actually happened to Rolf.

"Thank you, Mrs. Hein. I know this must be very stressful for you."

"Yes, I agree that it is stressful. I will call you and tell you what the police say to me." Agatha took down Mr. Agostino's phone number.

She planned to go to Rolf's real estate office soon. It was going to be difficult overcoming the staff's wonderment at her sudden transformation and surprisingly self-assured assumption of command.

She was sure Rolf had told stories about her, and that they had not been flattering. He was a braggart and a bully, and he would be proud of his superiority, and would not hesitate to point out his wife's shortcomings, her frumpy appearance, her cow-like stupidity.

But the police did not know her prior appearance or habits or reputation. They did not know that she knew about Linda. She would convey to the police the impression that to them would make sense: the intelligent, well-kept wife of a wealthy real estate baron, a woman who loved her husband, thought he loved her, and had no idea he was sleeping with his secretary.

She picked up the phone and dialed 911.

≈23≈

My appointment at the orthopedic clinic was very early, and it took me three times as long as usual to get showered and dressed and down to the car, but I had allowed for that.

I had slept for the last couple of nights on the big wide couch rather than in my wonderful comfortable bed; I had found out to my dismay that round-the-clock ice and elevation do not play nicely with sheets and covers.

The good news this morning was that the ankle did not hurt much. I skipped the Oxy when I woke up so I could safely operate the heavy machinery that is my car, and felt no worse off for the lack of painkillers.

I wore a long skirt and a sweater, plus one sock and running shoe. I had to tuck the skirt up into the neckline of my sweater to kneel-step-kneel-step down the stairs. I realized I would need more yoga pants; I could not comfortably roam San Francisco, the city of houses with a flight of steps to the front door, shoving the hem of my skirt into my collar. As Mater would say, it was *unseemly*.

Thorne called just before I headed out. Beth had come out of surgery; she was listed as stable and was recovering at Stanford. He and Don and Mr. Bonebreak's minions have been watching over the Ballantines. Apparently the hospital has cooperated with their round-the-clock presence, given Beth's gunshot wound. Thorne said Beth's parents were "ashen" and "subdued."

Thorne graduated from Choate and Princeton, with a little Harvard Business School thrown in for good measure, and from time to time his Ivy League vocabulary leaks out.

At the clinic I parked, got myself into the wheelchair with only one episode of crutches clattering to the ground, and started rolling. It was my first time out in the world on my own since the accident, and it was a glorious feeling to be out and mobile without needing anyone's help.

I rolled up the ramp and down the hall to the appointment desk. My arm muscles were a little sore from rolling and hoisting myself everywhere. So far no hand blisters, though, thanks to the gloves.

Dr. Saam will be my surgeon. His team of ex-tremely attractive orthopedic residents and nurse practitioners (what is it about orthopedics that pulls in the beauties?) took more pictures and ex-claimed at the perfect realignment of foot and an-kle that the ER doctor had achieved after his three valiant attempts to restore proper syndesmosis.

Syndesmosis. See how much new stuff I am learning! The upside of the smithereen fracture!

The docs described in glowing terms the posi-tive effect the perfect repositioning would have on my ability to heal, avoid arthritis, and walk without pain once the ankle fracture mended. It was reassuring to hear all that.

Nonetheless, when Dr. Yengar, one of the res-idents under Dr. Saam's tutelage, was explaining the surgery to me, I was suddenly overwhelmed. They were going to put in plates and screws on both sides of my ankle. It was going to be a per-manent installation. The ankle would not heal on its own without the hardware.

Nothing was going to be the same ever again in there. The scars would be long and deep. I would have to give up any hope of dancing Odile/Odette or Saturday Night Fevering with John Travolta. I have never felt the slightest incli-nation to do either, but still.

"What's the matter?" Dr. Yengar asked when my face turned red and my eyes went leaky on me.

"I'm feeling like I blew it. That I've damaged myself irrevocably, and carelessly, and for the rest of my life I'm going to be crippled."

I couldn't hold in a wave of emotion, grief tinged with self-pity, that took over. I was off the opiates and the repercussions of the damage I had done to myself had finally hit me. I took out a tissue and swabbed my eyes.

"Listen to me," he said. "It was an accident. Accidents happen to everybody."

He ducked down and looked up at me so that I couldn't avoid eye contact.

"Have you never had a broken bone before?"

"I may have broken a toe once. It hurt a lot and I had to tape one little piggy to its next-door little piggy."

He took my hand and pressed it for emphasis as he spoke.

"Then you have had a very long ride on the bus without a mishap, and you have been very lucky, and you were way overdue for something like this. Everybody gets hurt, mostly through no fault of their own.

"You do have a serious injury, and Dr. Saam is the Best in the West at putting ankles like yours back together so that they work properly ever after. We will take good care of you here. We are very good at our jobs. You do your part, and we will do ours, and you stop blaming yourself and focus on healing and doing the physical therapy when the time comes, and I promise you, you will be fine."

I could have kissed him. He was very handsome of course, being an orthopedist, which increased the kissability factor. But if he had looked like Freddy Krueger I could've kissed him anyway. Nevertheless, I held myself in check and sat up straight.

"How many times a day do you have to give that particular spiel?" I asked.

He laughed. "A couple dozen or so."

"Well, it was beautifully done. So okay, my job is to do what you tell me to do, and thank you and everyone who is helping me to get well, and just get on with it, yes?"

"Exactly."

He really had a lovely smile, did Dr. Yengar. There were dimples involved.

So I thanked him and after that I asked questions and took notes and focused on healing and being grateful.

Margaret, the scheduling nurse, put the bionicizing surgery on the calendar for Thursday of the next week. By then, they all agreed, the swelling should have subsided sufficiently to allow the surgery to proceed safely.

Until next Thursday then: ice and elevation, elevation and ice.

I drove home from the clinic and fixed myself a salad for lunch. The neighbors' morning activi-

ties—dog walking, jogging, driving to work—
were long since completed. Everything on 48th
Avenue was quiet.

My dogs and cats were sleeping in the various
sunny spots beneath the south-side windows of
the house. I had a cup of peppermint tea to sip
and a new book to read about Ulysses Grant and
Mark Twain. Who knew those two had been such
pals?

A police car pulled up in front of the Hein
house. Perhaps this had something to do with
why Mrs. Hein was suddenly driving the Mercedes and toting home a congregation of shopping bags from expensive stores.

I watched the officer ring the doorbell and
saw Mrs. Hein open the door and let her in. Or at
least I thought it was Mrs. Hein at first, but the
woman who opened the door had dark auburn
hair and was dressed like a mannequin.

What was going on over there?

I fell asleep.

≈2 4≈

Agatha invited the police officer, Debra Rodriguez, into the living room and asked her to sit in
the comfortable chair—Rolf's chair. She offered
coffee or tea or water, which Ms. Rodriguez declined.

"I need to ask some questions, Mrs. Hein, and
we need to complete some simple paperwork. Before I go it would be extremely helpful to have a
recent picture of your husband, if you have one."

"Yes, of course. Please tell me what I must do.
I would have called sooner but I did not know
whether I must wait a certain period, and sometimes my husband goes on business and does not
call, so at first I was not worried."

"In California there is no waiting period to report a missing person, Mrs. Hein. And given what

you told me on the phone, I think it's wise to fill out a report in this case. Shall we get started?"

"Yes, yes."

"First, I need to know some specifics about your husband."

Agatha answered the officer's questions about Rolf: his height and weight, age, eye and hair color, full name and spelling, work address, birthplace, cell phone number, when she had seen him last, where he had said he was going when he left—it went on for quite a few minutes.

The officer also asked for Rolf's credit card information; Agatha had prepared for that. She gave the officer different card numbers than the one she had been using, and explained that she was using a card that was in her husband's name but it was for her personal use. The officer did not seem to find that odd.

"Do you have any idea at all where your husband might have gone?" Officer Rodriguez asked. "Perhaps a trip home to Germany? Or to a family member or friend here in the U.S.?"

"He had no relatives in the States. I am not familiar with all his friends and business acquaintances. He was not close to his family in Germany. There were some cousins, I believe, but no brothers or sisters, and his parents are dead. I think you must look at his phone records and talk to his office staff."

Agatha was satisfied that any conversation

with the office staff would result in the revelation of Rolf's affair with Linda, and she felt confident that the police would believe Rolf had run away with his whore.

"We will do that. Can you call the office and let them know we will be in touch?"

"Mr. Agostino knows. He and I have spoken already. But I will go to the office and confirm your investigation with him and tell the staff you will be asking about my husband."

Agatha decided she had not sounded alarmed or upset enough during the conversation. She did not want to raise the officer's suspicions by being too calm.

"I am very concerned," she said. "It is not like my Rolf to not answer calls from the office. From me, yes, sometimes, but never from the office. I am very afraid something bad has happened."

"Mrs. Hein, we will pursue this case actively and notify other law enforcement agencies throughout the country that your husband is missing. We will forward his description and photograph to them, and we will monitor his phone and credit card use. We will do our best to find him and bring him home safely to you."

Officer Rodriguez paused. "I do not want to upset you, so please excuse me for asking this. In some cases, husbands have been known to walk away from marriages with no warning. Is that a possibility in this case, in your opinion?"

"I doubt it very much. He has left everything behind, and the bank accounts are intact. He is not a man of sudden actions. He is very careful and plans everything he does. We have been married many years and we are not honeymooners anymore, but I do not believe he would walk away without taking his money or his clothes."

The officer seemed satisfied. Agatha signed the finished paperwork and gave the officer a photo of Rolf from last year's office party, and that was that.

So easy, Agatha thought. She was proud of how she had handled herself during the interview. Poised but worried; that had been the right note to strike.

She determined to wait another day or two before going to the real estate office to see what other secrets Rolf had hidden from her. Soon enough it would be time to take control of the rest of Rolf's life.

≈25≈

I withstood the nonstop icing/elevating for two more days. By Friday morning I was as stir-crazy as any lifer at San Quentin. Also, the combination of large doses of egg salad, cheese from Yolanda's casserole, no physical exercise, and the intake of opiates had led to a certain cork-like suspension of peristalsis. Ahem.

I felt a profound need to go to the East-West Café and have some Krispy Ricey Yam Ringles and a Minty Chix Salada with soy dressing. Roughage.

I found myself wondering if anyone in San Francisco was in the business of delivering crate-loads of dried fruit to one's doorstep. Preferably coated with a thick layer of dark chocolate.

I felt the need to sit in the parking lot at the

end of Sloat Boulevard and stare at the Pacific Ocean, my favorite shrink, and solve some earth-shattering problems.

Like, why was I living the way I lived?

Why did I choose to take into my house a man who carried around violence in his daily arsenal of life behaviors? Whose clients were always in danger, which meant he was always in danger, which meant I was always in danger?

Why was I seemingly incapable of settling down with a slightly balding software engineer who lived in a Walnut Creek 2-BR 2-BA condo, and who would treasure a woman such as *moi*? Why could I not find a man who liked to read about Anton Chekhov as well as Spenser, who would love listening to Amos Lee and Cake and Bonnie Raitt and Anna Netrebko, and who would loath canned-laughter sitcoms? Who could adore a woman who shunned cooking and kept a great sufficiency of pets? A man who would ignore the fact that I kept a thug living in the basement? Who would love me in spite of the fact that from time to time I referred to myself as *moi* without any of that misguided Miss Piggy irony?

I answered my question, but I wasn't alto-gether happy with the answer: perhaps the thug living in the basement was that man, minus the software engineer/Walnut Creek condo elements.

Another question I contemplated: Why was it that, when I called my Mother to let her know I had broken my ankle and would be in surgery, she told me she had a golf tournament on that day and a luncheon the next, but would stop by after that? And perhaps she could take me to that new restaurant downtown that everyone was raving about?

"Doesn't that sound like fun?" she had said. "DeDe says it's divine." And then she said, "Tata, love, I'll call you very soon."

I am not kidding.

Because of Mater, I don't wonder why the other family members I love live so far away from each other.

My oldest brother, Brett, lives in Chicago. He trades hog futures, evidence indicates. He gets up very early every day to find out what exactly is going on with pigs everywhere in the known world. He seems to like doing that, and he certainly talks about hogs more than you would think possible. He is single; can you imagine?

Brett was sufficiently abashed, aghast really, to compensate for Mater's off-handedness, but he lives in Chicago, so brotherly aghastitude is all he can be expected to muster from the Midwest. There is not a surfeit of hogs housed within the city limits of San Francisco. Raccoons and skunks and opossums we have aplenty, but I am unaware of a skunk futures market should Brett decide to relocate back home.

Next oldest brother Collin lives in Santa Monica with his boyfriend. He immediately offered to come help out, which I declined, as he knew I would. He works in the movie business as a production designer, and was currently busy designing yet another comic book production, figuring out what exploding stuff should look like.

Collin and I share the staring-at-the-ocean thing and agree that more people should stare at oceans because it will inevitably lead to world peace. Or maybe just a nice nap, but it will be a peaceful rather than combative snooze.

Younger sister Eleanora lives with her husband and two children in Atlanta. She is the one who, struggling with the structure and length of it when she was a toddler, shortened my name from Alexandra to Xana. After our call I was expecting flowers from her; she loves to send flowers, for occasions or non-occasions. The flowers will be from Podesta Baldocchi and will totally rock and will last for many days, and I will love looking at them and thinking of her.

Youngest sister Louisa—Lulu—is single and lives in Carmel, not far from Mater in Pebble Beach. They are quite bonded, those two, she being the baby of the family, named for Mater and all that.

"I'm on my way," she said.

"No, sweetie, you are not. I'm fine."

"But what are you doing for company? I'm guessing the man-beast is on a job somewhere."

"Thorne is working, yes. But I am okay here. I'm all set up so I can go out whenever I want to. And it's San Francisco, so there are a zillion places I can order food from if I don't feel like going out. And Yolanda brought me some macaroni and cheese that I'm still working on, and will be for another month at least."

Lulu knows how I feel about cooking stuff. In my world, if you can't nuke it or toaster-oven it or eat it raw, then someone else is in charge of the food.

"Are you sure, Sis? I can be there in two hours."

"I'm sure, Button." Eleanora is not the only one who can dish out nicknames. We are WASPs, after all, and therefore riddled with nicknames. Lulu had in fact been very cute as a baby.

So it was left that I was to manage for myself, which was fine by me, really. Right now all I needed was a wee break from the ice and the ankle-elevating. Also from contemplating why it was that I could not select and keep a good man or have a closer family.

First things first: how to keep the damn crutches from falling over at every opportunity. It was too easy to just set them down lengthwise on the ground. I planned to continue conducting scientific inquiries into the nature of crutch stability, or the lack thereof.

Next, and somewhat more pressing: get back

down to Asa's office and talk to Marcus and Sergei, as well as Beth and Asa. Even, if he would allow it, their neurosurgeon father.

Something really wrong was going on with that company and that family. I was going to say not much, and be the pattern of all patience, and find out what that wrong something was, before a better-aimed bullet found its way into one of the twins.

Why did I believe this was this my task to take on? Here's why: My Dad was and my Mom is an alcoholic. There is nothing like a good old-fashioned drunk-raised codependent for fixing everyone else's problems and ignoring her own.

For your information, "Let's roll" takes on new significance when you're in a wheelchair.

≈2ȱ≈

Agatha wore the new violet pantsuit for her drive to Rolf's Atherton real estate office. She had never gone there on her own before. She did not call ahead to let them know she was coming.

Let us see what really goes on when the cat is away, she thought.

As she pulled into Rolf's parking space in front of the building, Phil Agostino opened the door to the office and, smiling broadly, walked toward the car. He stopped walking and smiling when he saw her step out.

Then he put the smile back on and walked over to her.

"Good morning, Mrs. Hein." Phil shook Agatha's hand with both of his, holding her hand for a moment in his before releasing it. Agatha interpreted this as a compassionate expression, an awareness that things were out of kilter and she required comforting.

"I thought you were Rolf for a moment there," he said, "and yet how could I make such a mistake. You've changed…" He caught himself before putting his foot entirely in his mouth. "You look lovely today, may I say," he finally managed to get out.

"You are kind, thank you," Agatha said, nodding slightly in acknowledgement of the compliment. She felt abashed by Phil's attention and averted her glance. Was this what other women experienced? Did they become accustomed to it? Take it in stride? She thought she would find out soon enough. She promised herself that from now on she would notice and relish every compliment she was lucky enough to be paid. She looked up at his eyes.

"The police came to the house the other morning and I made a report," Agatha said. "Has the officer spoken to anyone here yet?"

"Yes, but we've been waiting to hear from you about any news," he answered.

Agatha noticed that Mr. Agostino was standing between her and the door to the office, blocking her way.

"I thought it best to drive here and see what is going on in Rolf's office. I will look through his things and try to find some idea of what he has done."

Mr. Agostino hesitated. Agatha saw that he would prevent her if he could think of a reason to do so. She sidestepped around him.

"Please let the employees know I may have questions for them," she said firmly.

"Mrs. Hein, are you sure this is wise? Mr. Hein is quite…particular about his office."

Agatha walked to the office door and waited for Phil to pull it open for her.

"If anyone knows how particular Rolf is about his things, I am the one," she said.

"Yes, of course, but…"

Agatha stopped inside the door, next to Betsy's reception desk. She turned to Phil and, looking him in the eye, spoke quietly and with authority.

"Mr. Agostino. My husband has been missing for more than four days now. I need to attend to his affairs for him. Is there a reason I must not?"

Phil, caught short by Agatha's unexpectedly professional grooming, her shift from the mousy, unprepossessing housewife he recalled from office parties to this elegantly garbed powerhouse, said "There's no reason at all, Mrs. Hein. Let me show you to Mr. Hein's office." He turned to Betsy and asked for the key.

"We open his office for him every day, but we locked it again after we realized he wasn't coming in on Monday."

"Very wise. Thank you for your caution,"

Agatha said.

She could feel the stares of everyone at their desks along the walls as she walked to the back of the building where Rolf's enclosed office was. She saw out of the corner of her eyes the employees turning to whisper to each other.

About me, Agatha thought. *They cannot believe I look so nice.*

She stood up straight and walked confidently in her new shoes. Her hair was combed away from her face this morning, so everyone could see her attractive make-up.

Halfway to Rolf's office a small salt-and-pepper-colored dog stood up next to one of the agent's desks and stepped in front of Agatha. The nameplate on the desk said Patricia Solens.

"And who is this?" Agatha asked, bending to greet the dog, holding out her hand for him to sniff. "What a well-behaved boy you are not to jump up."

"I'm sorry, Mrs. Hein. I only brought the Kaiser to work because I'm trying to find a home for him, and Mr. Hein hasn't been in so I didn't think it would be a problem."

It was a miniature schnauzer, Agatha saw. "You call him the Kaiser?"

"Well, the name on his papers is Wilhelm Battenberg Von Hesse, so we just call him The Kaiser. He has that little beard, like the Kaiser had. Or sometimes we call him Billy."

"Why are you getting rid of him?" Agatha stroked the dog's rough fur, scratching behind his ears and under his throat. She felt that her wish for a pet to love had come true, and so quickly that it must have been foreordained.

She had always wanted a dog, but Rolf had not permitted it, saying dogs brought dirt into a house. As if the task of cleaning any of the dirt that came into Agatha's spotless home would ever fall to Rolf.

"It's not that we're getting rid of him at all. But we do need to find him a good home. We love him to death, but we're moving to England for my husband's job and we can't take him with us because of the quarantine there. And everyone we've asked so far wants a puppy. The Kaiser is three years old."

"I will take him," Agatha said, standing up. She saw the shock on the woman's face and thought perhaps she had spoken too peremptorily. "I would love to take him home with me," she said, softening her expression, smiling.

"But…"

"Yes?"

"Well, it was my understanding that Mr. Hein was allergic."

"Ah." Agatha had to think quickly. She was surprised that people at the office would know this about Rolf, that he would have admitted to his staff any personal frailties, because he had always seen his allergies as a weakness, a failing not to be tolerated, much less publicly acknowledged.

"Well, I will make a special place for the little Kaiser so that he will not bother Rolf."

It was all Agatha could think of to say in the moment. She wanted the dog very much, but she realized she had made a mistake.

"Are you sure? I would hate to think of him being kept outside, or isolated. He's a family pet and he's used to being with people. We have children who pay him a lot of attention and play with him."

"My home is across the street from a park, and there are many people who walk their dogs there every day. He would have lots of friends. And when Rolf is not at home I would keep him with me."

That sounded better, Agatha thought.

"He's a terrier," Patricia said. "He's not that good with other dogs. He doesn't fight so much as he bristles. You just have to hold his leash firmly and tell him 'Off' and he behaves himself. He's very well trained, really."

Agatha realized everyone in the office was listening. Phil was at the door to Rolf's office holding the door open.

"Let's talk about this in private, yes?" she said, gesturing at Rolf's office. "And bring the Kaiser so he and I can have a nice chat, yes?"

"Um, Mrs. Hein?" Phil said, standing by the door to Rolf's office.

"Yes?"

"Rolf locks his desk and credenza. I don't have a key for those. He always kept those keys with him rather than here in the office."

"But where is Linda? Does she not keep the keys also?"

Agatha thought this was a brilliant move. *Let's see what he does now*, she thought.

"Since Rolf is not here, she is taking a few days off," Phil said. "And we can't find her keys, so perhaps she has them with her." He was so obviously lying that Agatha just nodded her head.

"I have a set of keys," Agatha said. "But I would have thought with Rolf gone his assistant would be making sure everything was handled correctly."

Phil gave her a look Agatha could not interpret. "Well, this time she put me in charge so she could take a few well-deserved days off. She's been working very long hours recently. But I wasn't aware that Rolf had another set of keys. I thought there were only the two sets."

Agatha felt herself blush and strove to quell a wave of nervous emotion. She felt her underarms prickle.

"My Rolf is so careful. He keeps extra keys for everything on a rack in the garage," she said, smiling, holding up the keys, which she had found in Rolf's pants pocket. *Thank God I removed his initialed key fob*, she thought, *or Phil would surely have recognized it*.

"Of course," Phil said. Agatha could see she had done the right thing. Phil had clearly wondered how Agatha could have a set of Rolf's desk keys if there were only two sets and Rolf always kept his set with him and Linda had the other set.

Once in Rolf's office, seated behind the desk and petting the dignified little dog, Agatha finally was able to convince Patricia that she was serious about adopting Wilhelm and that she would give the dog a loving home.

Patricia spent many minutes explaining what food the Kaiser liked, how often he had to be exercised and for how long, what commands he would respond to, and what his favorite toys were.

Agatha had to promise to order a new identification tag for the dog's collar, with her phone number and the dog's name. Patricia said the dog's vaccinations were current, and that he had an implanted identification chip. She said she would update the chip's information with the Palo Alto veterinarian who gave the Kaiser his shots.

Once it had been agreed that Agatha would take the dog, she wanted to take him home right away, before Patricia changed her mind. While Patricia left the office to drive home and fetch the dog's things, Agatha spent a hurried half hour rifling the drawers of Rolf's desk and credenza.

As she had expected, everything was well organized, and Agatha found it easy to locate what she was looking for. In a side drawer of the desk she found two more checkbooks: one personal and one for the office accounts. In a tall cabinet she found file folders containing bank statements for both. She lifted out the most recent statement for each account.

She could not ask Rolf's assistant for help finding the current real estate files, since Rolf's assistant was buried in the back yard under the Baccara hybrid tea roses.

Agatha quickly grabbed all the files from Rolf's desk drawer and from the rack on Linda's desk, shoving them into the black leather tote she had bought at Nordstrom.

She asked Phil if there were any urgent bills or other financial matters that required her immediate attention.

"Oh, Jeannie handles all that. There's nothing pressing just now. And Jeannie does the payroll, which is all direct deposit."

In the end, Agatha loaded up the Mercedes with the Kaiser's bed, toys, dry and canned food, pet crate, plastic raincoat, halter, and a set of holiday collars with pumpkins, Christmas wreaths, shamrocks, and stars and stripes. Agatha remembered the blue bin on the shelf above Rolf's workbench. It would be perfect for holding all the Kaiser's things.

Agatha said goodbye to everyone, thanked Patricia and, promising again to take the best care in the world of the Kaiser, walked the dog on his leash to the car.

The dog jumped right into the front seat. She let him sit there because Agatha could not bring herself to put him in his crate while driving, as Patricia had instructed her to.

When Agatha saw that the dog had to stand on his hind legs to see out of the window, she reached across and used the seat controls to raise the seat until the dog could get a good view sideways and out of the windshield without standing.

"Sit!" she commanded. Wilhelm sat. Agatha stroked his head. "Good boy," she said.

She was anxious to get home and go through the bank information and the real estate files. She wanted to see how many more millions of dollars Rolf had hidden from her.

And she wanted to throw the squishy ball for the little Kaiser to fetch. She wanted to hug him and let him lick the make-up off her face. She wanted to give Wilhelm Battenberg Von Hesse a doggy biscuit. Lots of biscuits. She wanted to see his love for her shining from his eyes.

≈2 7≈

I called Thorne. Herewith the conversation:

"Hi."

"Hi. I need to talk to them all again. The sooner the better."

"Good."

"Can you arrange it?"

"Yes."

"Where should I drive to first?"

"Here. Room 512."

"Here" was the hospital then.

"Are you allowed to use cell phones in the hospital?"

"No."

End of conversation.

I found Thorne and Asa in Beth's room. Beth was in the bed, awake and full of tubes into and out of her shoulder. Don and Bix Bonebreak's minions were nowhere to be seen.

Thorne read my unspoken question. "Off-duty."

I wheeled over to Asa's chair and, when he got up, stood up on one leg to hug him.

"Hi," I said to Beth, reseating myself and wheeling to her bedside.

"Hi."

"When does the doctor say you can go home?"

"Tomorrow."

"How soon before you can be up and around?" What I meant was "When do you plan to go back to the office?"

"A week," she said, understanding the intent of the question, "but I'll probably go back to work sooner than that."

"How do you feel about that?"

"I think if someone wants to kill you they will eventually kill you. So I am going to act like nobody wants to kill me, and I'll keep Don or Thorne or the ugly stepbrothers Thorne added to the team around me to make sure it doesn't happen."

"Okay," I said. "Can we talk about the other day, please?"

"I told the police and I'm telling you, I couldn't see anything outside. It was dark."

"A flash? A sound that would indicate direction?"

"No. I wasn't really looking at anything. I just wanted to see how dark it had gotten outside. I didn't really have a reason for it." She paused and looked down at her hands, one of them taped with an IV running into the vein. "I was upset about my Dad's behavior, and I didn't want to look at the walls of that conference room anymore."

"Beth," I said after a moment, "what do you think happened?" I was dodging the real question I thought she knew the answer to: Who do you think shot you?

"I don't know. I really don't. The police asked me all this and I really have no idea who could have done it."

I didn't believe her. She was in charge of the administration of BioMorphic Technologies, and a partner in the enterprise. She was a physician, highly educated, astute and experienced. The fact that we are smart and have gone to pricey schools does not necessarily make us willing to face the truth about ourselves or our families.

My inner voice said, *Take her somewhere her father isn't. She came out of her childhood surgery the correct gender. She loves her father and he loves her.* I couldn't bring myself to suggest that her father had shot her.

"Is there anyone who would want to hurt you or the company? Who is angry about anything? A resentful ex-employee perhaps? I know your Dad was angry when I met him, but I'm thinking of anyone else who might have a grudge against you or your brother."

"Do you think someone was trying to shoot my brother instead of me?"

"I'm just asking questions, trying to figure out what happened. You only pulled back the curtain for a moment, and you and Asa were dressed similarly on Tuesday. You were in silhouette, with the conference room light behind you, and the two of you look very much alike."

"Shit," said Asa. He and Beth stared at each other.

"Did the police ask you about this possibility?" I said.

"No. One detective talked to Beth after the surgery and the other one talked to me in the waiting area," Asa said. "The two of them never saw us together, and they never suggested I might have been the target."

"They may have come up with that theory in the meantime, Asa. Have they been back to talk to either of you since Tuesday?"

"No."

"If they do, or even if they don't, you should tell them about this," I said.

"Yes. Because we haven't fired anyone, so there are no disgruntled ex-employees," Asa said. "I can't imagine that anyone else would have any reason to hurt either of us."

"Neither can I," said Beth.

I swiveled the chair around to look at Thorne. "When are the troops back on duty?"

"Two." It was one-thirty.

We waited for them. I rolled away from Beth's bedside, and Asa shifted his chair to take my place next to her. The twins talked about what to do at BioMorphic Tech in the coming few days. They spoke to each other in biotech-speak, which I have not mastered. DeLeon would have understood them, but they might as well have been chatting in Farsi in my case.

Thorne and I sat, amicably silent, listening to them. For all I know he understood what they were going on about just fine, but did not feel the need to say so. Thorne almost never feels the need to say so.

When Don arrived back at two on the dot, Thorne, Asa and I left the hospital and headed to BioMorphic Technologies' headquarters. Thorne and I drove separately; after scanning the parking lot in all directions and then helping me into my car, Thorne drove Asa in his BMW.

Once parked at the company's office, I felt like being upright in lieu of rolling. I left the wheelchair in the car and used the crutches to hop into the lobby and down the aisle to the conference room.

The glass wall had been repaired and the vertical blinds were open, the afternoon sunlight streaming into the warm room. Thorne pulled the blinds shut and closed the conference room door.

Settled into a chair with my foot on the adjacent seat, elevated and iced, I was going to ask Asa to locate and retrieve Sergei and Marcus, if they were on-site. But before I could ask, I saw the strangest thing.

Marching down the aisle outside the conference room were a loud Dr. Frank Ballantine and a purple-suited, auburn-haired Agatha Hein. Mrs. Hein was walking some kind of small terrier, who was heeling like a champ, his head high and his perky paws moving briskly along the beige industrial carpeting.

"They are violating the terms of the lease and the zoning for this business park," Frank said loudly, pointing ahead of him to the lab area. "You can see for yourself the laboratory where employees are engaged in life sciences research. The zoning is quite clear that no biological research is to be conducted in this facility. This site is limited to technological activity only."

Thorne had moved to the doorway and stood blocking it as Frank passed. The elder Dr. Ballantine was turned away and focused on Mrs. Hein, and he failed to see Thorne or me or his son in the conference room.

"I need to hear this," Asa said, on his feet and walking to the door.

"Stay here." Thorne held up his hand.

"I have to talk to him."

"Thorne will bring him to you, Asa," I said. "He wants to be able to control the environment where you two talk to each other."

"Oh."

Asa sat down. Thorne opened the door, turning to the right to follow Frank and Agatha's voices.

We heard Dr. Ballantine shout, *"You!"* and then Mrs. Hein's startled, German-accented exclamations, accompanied by a few sharp barks.

Thorne walked in holding Dr. Frank by both arms. Dr. Frank was not happy about that, but verbal and physical protestations are in vain when plied against Thorne, so the doctor wound up sitting in a chair where Thorne put him. Frank was huffy as hell about it, but he sat. Thorne stood between Frank and Asa.

"Hello Mrs. Hein," I said, waving to her when she peeked into the room. She was clutching the black and gray rough-coated dog against her chest.

"I'm Alexandra Bard. We live across the street from each other in San Francisco."

"Yes, I know you," she said, stepping into the room and giving Thorne a look as she stood back at what I am guessing she considered a safe distance from him.

"I saw you were hurt the other day," she said to me.

"Yes, but I'm doing much better now. Do you mind my asking what brings you to these offices today? It's such a surprise to see you here."

"My husband's company leases this property. I was just at Rolf's office and I was driving home when Dr. Ballantine called me and insisted I turn around and come here immediately. He said the occupants were breaking the law. My husband is—not available. So I am handling things right now."

"My son's company is violating the zoning regulations," Dr. Ballantine insisted loudly, pointing his finger at Agatha. "You are legally responsible for evicting them forthwith."

"Even if this company is doing something incorrect, Dr. Ballantine, I do not see how an eviction is so very urgent. You told me that I must come here right away with you. But now I do not see that I have a responsibility to do anything right away. If there is a zoning error, you must take it up with the county and they will decide. If they decide it is necessary, then I will proceed to an eviction. I do not see this as a problem for my real estate company until the zoning issue has been settled."

Mrs. Hein held the dog in front of her, a canine shield in the face of Ballantine's temper.

I was impatient with this conversation. I never for a moment considered what might transpire after I asked what I asked next. Sometimes I am more than a little misguided in my attempts to arrive at the truth.

I attribute this misguided urge for honesty, no matter the cost, to my upbringing, during which I was surrounded by drunks who persisted in telling me they were not drunk, at the same time their vodka-drenched exhalations were scorching my eyebrows.

"Dr. Ballantine," I said, "why are you so determined to stop your children's research? What is it about their work here that offends you so much that you would shoot your own daughter?"

There was a moment of silence. Thorne was the one who spotted what was about to happen, and he reached for Frank just as Frank erupted.

Frank, a polished, supremely educated product of expensive schools and increasingly demanding professional health environments where he was treated like a god, made a noise somewhere between a growl and a shriek and launched himself across the table at me, arms outstretched. I admit it was very shocking.

Thorne caught him by the shoulders and hauled him backward into the chair again. Asa pushed his own chair away from the table into the corner, as far from his father as he could get.

Agatha Hein ran to the door and out of the room, carrying the yipping dog as she raced toward the lobby. She did not come back.

"Dad?" Asa said from the corner.

"Don't call me that ever again." Frank stared at his son with eyes as dull and black as chimney soot. "You are not my son anymore."

"Dad, I never was your son."

Asa's anguish was so pronounced that I shook my head at his father in disgust.

"There was never anything of this sort in my family. What you are trying to do will destroy your mother."

"Actually Mom is okay with it. I've talked to her."

"You told your mother about this and she did not tell me?"

"She told me she never wanted to turn me into a boy. It's you who wanted a son. That's why we kept all of this from you. Because we were afraid you would react the way you have. And now look at you."

"There was never anything of this sort in my family," Frank repeated.

"Dad, you are a physician. You are educated enough to know that what happened to Beth and me can happen to any family."

"Not to me."

Asa stood up, faced his father, and spoke with authority. "But it didn't happen to you. It happened to Beth and to me. You and Mom made the best choice you thought you could at the time. I don't blame you for it. Back then it was impossible to know better what to do."

Asa shrugged.

"Under those circumstances, people make the best decision they can, and sometimes it's the right one and sometimes they live to regret what they've done. But Beth and I are doing work here that can help people like us—people of every kind—all over the world. So that parents like you and Mom will never have to make a wrong decision again."

Asa walked closer to the table, closer to the father who was rejecting him.

"I don't care how you try to justify it," Frank said. "What you're doing will bring nothing but shame and embarrassment to your mother and me, and *I won't have it, do you hear me*?"

Thorne stepped between Dr. Ballantine and Asa, blocking the father's view of his son. Frank looked up at Thorne's face.

"You shot Beth," Thorne said to Frank.

"I didn't mean to."

"You were trying to shoot me?" Asa said, his authoritative tone gone and heartbreaking plaintiveness replacing it.

"Without you, Beth couldn't have continued the research." Frank leaned around Thorne to point his finger at Asa. "You're the scientist; she's the business end of this. Without you the company would have folded, and we as a family would have mourned you and moved on."

Asa was stopped short by that. How do you

not get silenced by your father's admission that he wants to kill you? That your father thinks a family in mourning for you is more desirable than an intact family with a living child?

Asa's expression was stoic, but he slumped as he walked to the spaceport-shaped conference phone in the center of the table. Tapping a button, he heard a dial tone and hit four more buttons.

"Elena," he said, his voice again resolved and strong, "call nine-one-one please. Tell them we have the person who shot Beth here and to get here fast, sirens and lights."

Frank Ballantine stood up to run. Thorne had him confined in the chair again before I could swing my crutch at the monster's head and bean him into submission. I felt the almost uncontrollable urge to pound him with the crutch anyway.

When the police arrived four minutes later, Asa had rounded up two burly scientists—who knew there were burly scientists?—to stand guard over his father and Thorne had slipped down the hallway and out to his car.

When the white-coated scientist guards had been summoned to block the exit from the conference room, I hopped past them to a cubicle just outside, not wanting to get caught up in the questioning.

Frank made it past the two guards once, but I stuck out my crutch at ankle level and he went down like a tree. I think he was only bruised, but with luck maybe something important broke in enough places to be comminuted.

When the police arrived I waited until they were in the conference room taking custody of Frank before hopping out of the building to my car. I drove home behind Thorne.

We agreed that the East-West café sounded perfect as the site for a muted celebration. I ate a horseradish-laden entrée, which turned out to be a peristalsis stimulant *par excellence*.

Ahem.

≈28≈

I couldn't get over the change in Mrs. Hein. From the command post chair where I was faithfully elevating and icing I watched her drive down the street each morning in the Mercedes, her new dog sitting alertly in the passenger seat.

I hadn't talked to her since seeing her at the BioMorphic offices. It took some getting used to, her hairstyle that was no longer the sad mousy ponytail, her outfits that were no longer droopy cotton dresses and scuffed, sensible shoes.

Two days after my surgery, when I was back on painkillers and sporting a new cast, Thorne carried me downstairs and wheeled me into Sutro Park so I could be outdoors for some of the warm-ish noontime weather.

Theoretically I should have been icing and elevating nonstop, and for the most part I was being a compliant patient and doing what I had been told to do. Just for a bit though, I needed to smell the cypress trees and be out in the fresh midday air.

Thorne had Hawk and Kinsey on their leashes and was ambling with them around the pathways, letting them sniff as long as they wanted to.

Frank Ballantine was in jail, bail denied because he represented an imminent threat to his children. Asa and Beth were back at work and safe now.

From across 48th Avenue the Hein's garage door slid open. The white reverse lights of the Mercedes were lit, as were the red brake lights, when suddenly the little gray terrier scampered past the car and across the street into the park.

Mrs. Hein stopped the car, opened the door, called out a number of things loudly, none of which I understood, and came running after the dog.

As she came closer I heard what I thought was "Vilhelm! Kaiser! Billy! Nein! Nein! Off! Off!"

The dog was carrying something dark and bulky in his mouth as he ran. He looked very happy to be carrying it, and delighted to be chased.

I heard Hawk's deep woof as the terrier came right up to my wheelchair, a disgusting blob of dark something in his mouth. Wilhelm stopped in front of me and wagged his stumpy tail energetically back and forth.

Mrs. Hein ran toward us, yelling frantically.

I reached into my dog-walking jacket pocket for a small yellow puppy biscuit. I showed the terrier the biscuit. "Sit," I said. I really was just trying to keep him with me until Mrs. Hein could catch up to him and grab his collar.

Focusing on the puppy biscuit, he sat. I heard Thorne and the dogs running fast toward me from where they had been, not far from The Lions at the park entrance.

I held the puppy biscuit very high; I found I did not want to put my hand near the dog's mouth and feed it to him. I didn't want to throw the biscuit either, and have him run away. I was very afraid that the dog would jump up to get the biscuit and drop what he was carrying into my lap, but he didn't.

He set his trophy down carefully on the ground and looked back up again at the biscuit. He was panting, smiling a happy doggy smile under his bushy dirt-smudged whiskers, and wagging his stubby tail.

I don't remember the next part so well. I was making noises again, a little like when I had fallen and broken my ankle.

On the grass in front of me, dropped by Wilhelm the miniature schnauzer, was a human foot.

A decomposing and rather petite human foot, sporting a glimmer of coral toenail polish. I had seen enough foot x-rays recently to be quite certain of what I was looking at, even in the disturbing condition this foot presented itself in. Most of the dirt and bugs and worms had been shaken off during the dog's dash across the street. That was something to be grateful for, I guess.

Thorne and Agatha arrived from different directions. She bent down and scooped up her dog. His hind feet pedaled until she put an arm under them to hold them still.

She stared at the foot. She stared at me with her pale blue wolf eyes. She thanked me for stopping Wilhelm. She turned her attention to the dog.

"You are a naughty, naughty *schatzi*," she said, laughing, tapping her finger on his nose. She walked away scolding him.

"You must not dig in the garden. *Nein nein nein, mein kuschelbär, mein schnuckelchen.*"

She left the foot behind her on the ground and, cooing German endearments, walked calmly back to her house while her pet whimpered and squirmed in her arms. The dog seemed desperate to get back to his unearthed treasure.

Thorne stood next to me holding my straining dogs, who, as dogs always do, wanted nothing more than to meet another dog.

At some point Hawk and Kinsey switched

their attention to the revolting foot, and Thorne pulled them a safe distance away.

I was transfixed by the foot, especially the glint of toenail polish.

Thorne finally said, "Xana. Make the call."

I spoke to a brusque and somewhat skeptical 911 operator and, rolling myself a respectful but proprietary distance away from a foot that was in distinctly worse shape than mine, watched Thorne and the dogs drift silently backward into the trees toward home as soon as three squad cars came squealing to a stop in front of the park.

≈2 9≈

Thorne and I were sitting, amicably silent and the pattern of all patience, on the back yard deck. We gazed at the Prussian blue Pacific as the afternoon sun settled toward the horizon. The sky above us was delphinium blue. White fog stretched flat across the water ten miles out, like a layer of heavy cream on Irish coffee.

Thorne and I each held a mug of tea: his English Breakfast, mine Darjeeling. The day was still warm enough for me to leave my jacket draped across the back of my chair.

Asa and Beth had made me a holder of stock options, should there ever be a BioMorphic Technologies IPO. I was also a holder of Thorne's options, since ownership of such things requires one to be back on the grid, visible to the world.

Thorne had bought some more gold with the cash Asa paid him and had parked it safely in his money bin.

The docs had removed my post-surgery cast. My left ankle was snugly Velcroed into a big black boot. I was resting the boot on the lower rung of the railing, next to where the crutches leaned.

I continued to be engaged in crutch stability research. This time the pointy end was up, the armrest end down on the decking. I was betting that in less than five minutes a light breeze would cause the crutches to fall over, and that the clatter of their fall would scatter the napping cats.

The miraculous reconstruction of my ankle, the tools of healing available now to medical teams, the x-ray with its unsettling but amazing image of the titanium plates and screws holding my shattered bones together, all had me thinking about the Magician card: Hermes, the healer.

I know that the tools of transformation and healing are not exclusively physical. Friendship, affection, kindness, loyalty, honesty, steadfast-ness, all are resources that can help to mend the visible and invisible damage in us. Just as oppres-sion, harsh words, cruelty, sarcasm, lies, cynicism and disdain can inflict injuries that never fully heal.

Love, the most magnificent of the transforma-tional tools available in the universe, takes myriad guises, and can and does produce downright magical outcomes.

I was aware that my self-imposed isolation, my conscious resistance to encouraging and expressing love, had been more damaging to me than I had thought it could be.

I had conceived of my refusal to risk love, my insistence on stifling this most important resource and allowing it to atrophy, as a way of protecting myself.

But I knew very well that recusing myself from love—from life in fact—was not self-protection; it was cowardice. The path to mastery of tools is practice, not avoidance.

A tanker full of fuel processed at Chevron's Richmond Refinery headed out of the Golden Gate across water the sun had refracted into a shimmering quarter-mile-wide platter of polished silver.

"I am unaccustomed to being durably loved," I said.

Thorne looked at me. I looked at the ship.

"I have made it my habit to be adored and then abandoned," I said.

I stared at the fog, so far away, so pale, lying flat across the farthest edge of the Earth.

"Why aren't you with someone?" I asked without looking at Thorne.

"I am with someone," he said.

I elected to misunderstand him.

Thorne said nothing, the pattern of all patience, watching me not watch him.

He held his hand out. I saw his hand in my peripheral vision. I did not take it. He held his outstretched hand steady, waiting.

"Why does becoming lovers always have to be my decision?" I said. "I have not been any good at choosing."

I heard the frustration in my voice and took a deep breath to dispel it.

"The word for when a man insists on being a woman's lover without her consent is generally associated with a mandatory jail sentence and the loss of his right to vote," he said. "Not that I ever plan to vote."

Such an effusion of words. I was surprised to hear him string more than a handful together at once. His hand was rock solid, halfway across the open space between our chairs.

"A few months after my boyfriends dump me they tend to call and apologize for having bailed. My dreary wounded birds call and tell me I'm wonderful and declare what fools they were to let me go. It's because they have immediately fallen back into disrepair."

"Men seldom realize how essential it is to let an organized, capable, sweet-tempered woman care for them until they find one willing to do the job. After that, if they have half the sense God gave pocket lint, they hold on for all they're worth. Men are imbeciles if they don't treat a wonderful woman like the godsend she is."

"Whew," I said. "Gort."

We sat in some more amicable silence. Thorne's hand was waiting there in between us. He continued to be the pattern of all patience.

"I am not in disrepair," Thorne said finally. Out of the corner of my eye I saw him glance at my big black boot.

"But I am a ruffian," he said, "and mostly mute, and everyone except you is afraid of me."

"As they should be."

In my peripheral vision I saw him smiling at my profile, showing big handsome white teeth.

"And you are wonderful," he said. "A god-send."

I stared at the fog-blanketed horizon.

"Courage," Thorne whispered, the way the French say it: coo-RAAZH, the second G soft like it is in "garage."

I took another deep breath in, letting it out slowly.

The cool afternoon breeze gusted suddenly and the crutches fell clanking to the deck.

The napping cats jerked awake and scattered.

I reached out and Thorne took my hand into his.

Bevan Atkinson, author of *The Tarot Mysteries* including *The Fool Card, The Magician Card, The High Priestess Card,* and *The Empress Card,* lives in the San Francisco Bay Area and is a long-time tarot card reader.

Bevan currently has no pets but will always miss Sweetface, the best, smartest, funniest dog who ever lived, although not everyone agrees with Bevan about that.

Made in the USA
San Bernardino, CA
11 May 2018